BESSIE HOLLAND HECK has been a free-lance writer since 1946. With her first book, *Millie,* she won second place in the 1963 Sequoyah Children's Book Awards. *The Hopeful Years* followed in 1964, and in 1965 she wrote her first book for boys, *Cactus Kevin.* A lifetime resident of Oklahoma, Mrs. Heck writes vividly of the country and the people of her native state. She now lives in Tulsa with her husband and they have five children.

THE YEAR AT BOGGY

THE WORLD PUBLISHING COMPANY

CLEVELAND AND NEW YORK

The Year at Boggy

BESSIE HOLLAND HECK

Illustrated by Paul Frame

Published by The World Publishing Company
2231 West 110th Street, Cleveland 2, Ohio
Published simultaneously in Canada by
Nelson, Foster & Scott Ltd.
Library of Congress catalog card number: 66-13899
CO66
Designed by Jack Jaget

To Gaylia, my daughter

Contents

THE YEAR AT BOGGY

A Long-legged Pup

On her way through the front room Millie stopped and watched Mama lift the braided rugwork out of the cardboard workbox.

"Mama, do you think you'll be happy here?" Millie asked.

Mama was a serious-minded woman—not sad, but serious—and when she smiled it was as if a bright candle had been lit in a dim room. She smiled now, as much with her deep blue eyes as with her lips. "Yes, child. I think I could be happy here the rest of my days."

"Happiness is where you are," Millie said. "And since this is where we are, this is where I'm going to be happy, too."

Still smiling, Mama said, "I guess that's one way of putting it." She spread the small oval of rug on the floor and took the long tail of braid up in her lap. "I hope to finish this before long. I want to put it right here in front of the fireplace."

"It'll be pretty there." Millie went out on the front porch, picked up her jump rope and went down the steps and along the stone walk toward the gate.

"One . . . two . . . three . . . four . . ."   She counted as she skipped the flying rope, and all the while she looked down the road in the direction of the schoolhouse. It was only a mile and a half to school, and Papa had said she and her little sister Ruth might start next Monday.

But she dreaded starting a new school without her brothers. Always before, Theron, who was fifteen, and Charles, who was thirteen, had started with the girls. This time they'd have to start by themselves, for Papa needed the boys to help with the farm work. But what bothered Millie most was that she didn't yet know which grade she'd start in.

"Thirteen . . . fourteen . . . fifteen . . ."   Her blond braids bounced up and down on her shoulders. A wagon topped the rise, and letting the rope go limp, Millie waited till she was sure it was Papa and Theron. Then she gave herself a final burst of hot pepper, tossed the rope aside, and ran to the gate that led from the main road to the barn. With much pulling and pushing, she opened the heavy gate and stood aside while Papa drove through.

"Hi, Papa. We hoped you'd get back before sundown."

"Yes, we made it." Papa stopped the wagon and Theron climbed down. He held a long-legged pup in his arms. Papa drove on to the barn with the load of plows and other farm equipment.

"What's that!" Millie exclaimed, pointing at the overgrown pup. "And where's Bulger?"

Charles and Ruth ran up.

"This is Blue," Theron said. "I traded ole Bulger for him."

"You what!" The other three Holliway children all spoke at once.

"Just don't get excited." Theron put the dog down and took a shorter hitch on the rope about its neck. "I'll explain if you'll just give me time."

Trixie ran up, and the pup wailed as if she'd chewed his ear. "It's all right now," Theron said, patting both dogs. "You'll get acquainted in no time at all, and you'll just get along fine."

Millie, Charles, and Ruth looked impatiently at Theron.

"Some people by the name of Williams moved into our old place," Theron explained. "They had a mammy dog and three of these pups and I traded ole Bulger for this one." He stroked the pup's smoky-blue coat.

"Why?"

"Because ole Bulger was getting too fat and lazy to hunt," Theron said. "Besides, I've always wanted a hound pup that I could train to hunt just the way I want him to."

Millie shrugged. Bulger was Theron's dog . . . and she guessed he could do as he pleased with him. "What did Bulger think about it?" she asked.

"Ha," Theron snorted. "You should have seen him. He was so happy to get back to the old place that I don't think he would've come home with us if we'd wanted him to."

Children and dogs turned toward the yard.

"Son, where did you get that?" Mama asked, coming out on the back porch. Theron had to explain all over again.

As Theron told Mama about his and Papa's trip back to the old place, Millie shaded her eyes against the setting sun and saw the milk cows coming across the sloping pasture beyond the house.

Only last week the Holliways had left their home in the Kiamichi Mountains and had spent two days and a night on the road moving to this place southeast of Atoka, Oklahoma. They had been able to bring all their possessions with them in the two wagons except a load of farm implements, and Papa and Theron had gone back for those. It was November, 1912, and the brown leaves in the thicket of oaks at the corner of the back yard rustled in the wind. The peach and apple trees in the orchard south of the house were already bare.

Later, at the supper table, the family talked about the two places: the one they'd moved from in the mountains, and this one here in the bend of Muddy Boggy Creek. This place had a better house and a better barn, and Papa said it had some of the best farm land in the state. Papa was a tenant farmer and he was always looking for a better place for his family. For as long as Millie could remember, they had moved every fall. Sometimes they were near a school and sometimes not. So what she liked best about this place was that it was close to school.

The first farm Papa had heard about for rent near Atoka had a four-room house on it, but when Mama said she thought they should settle near a school, Papa said there was another place he could rent. Apparently this was the other place, for this house had only two large rooms and a lean-to built all the way across the back. In order to make a bedroom for Theron and Charles, Mama ripped apart some worn cotton sacks, washed the material, and then stitched the pieces together to make a heavy curtain across one end of the lean-to. The kitchen was at the other end. Millie loved Papa for having rented the place close to school.

"Papa, the other people sure moved into our old place fast, didn't they?" Millie said, buttering a biscuit.

"Yes," Papa answered. "When a landlord learns that a renter doesn't plan to stay another year he starts looking for another renter. We gave the landlord full notice, so he had another family ready to move in as soon as we moved out."

"Oh," Millie said thoughtfully. "Then did someone move out of this place just before we moved in?"

"Yes. We would have moved sooner if we hadn't had to wait for the other people to move out."

When Mama and the girls had finished the dishes, they joined Papa in the front room. The evening was cool, and a small fire burned in the fireplace. As Mama took up her rugwork, Papa looked at her over his newspaper.

"Well, Sarah, I see you have everything pretty well in place," he remarked.

"You know me, John," Mama answered. "I can't

settle down to anything till I know where everything is."

Holding the braid for Mama, Millie thought this would be a good time to discuss her problem about school. But Papa went back to his reading and Mama was intent again on her rugwork, so Millie just sat and thought about her problem all by herself.

Last spring Papa had needed Theron and Charles to help with the plowing, so the children had had to drop out of school long before the term was over. That meant they had not had a chance to finish their grades. Millie had been in the fifth grade only a few weeks, but she hoped that her teacher here in the new school wouldn't know this, for she was thinking strongly about skipping to the sixth grade. Ruth hadn't finished the second grade, but Ruth didn't seem to worry about school, one way or another.

Although Millie wanted desperately to start in the sixth grade on Monday morning, she was afraid she might not be able to do the work. And even if she could, would it be completely honest? She had worried about the matter for a long time without coming to a decision, so she guessed she'd better discuss it with Mama and Papa. But as she started to speak, Papa suddenly folded his newspaper and laid it aside.

"You children run along," Papa said. "I'm tired out and I want to go to bed."

Mama's and Papa's bed was in the front room, so now Millie and Ruth had to go to the kitchen or to their own bedroom. As they rose to leave, Mama said, "Girls, be sure to wash your feet before you go to bed."

"Yes, ma'am."

Theron and Charles had been out with the dogs and now they came into the kitchen.

"Is Blue going to be all right?" Millie asked.

"He's going to be fine," Theron answered proudly. "And just as soon as he gets used to us we're going to take him hunting."

After Millie had heated a pan of water and washed her feet, she went to her bedroom. Under the side of the bed there were two stacks of books. She had sorted all the fifth-grade books into one stack and all the sixth-grade books, which Charles had used last year, into another. This was Saturday night, and sometime between now and Monday morning she must make up her mind which stack she would use. She blew out the kerosene lamp, hopped into bed beside Ruth, and drew her feet up inside her flannel nightgown. She went to sleep quite undecided as to which books she'd pick up Monday morning.

A Problem at School

So many questions churned in Millie's mind that she scarcely knew what she was doing. Would they have a man teacher or a woman teacher? Should she wear last year's too-small shoes and be uncomfortable all day, or should she go barefoot and be embarrassed if all the other children had worn shoes? She was nearly beside herself with the secret burden of it all.

But the question that bothered her most was: Should she start in the sixth grade? She was afraid to ask anybody this late; what if they told her not to do it? What if they made her repeat the fifth? She couldn't bear it—twelve years old and still in fifth grade!

While scrubbing her neck and ears, Millie decided to tackle the sixth. With her decision made, she felt a lot better as Mama combed and braided her hair. Mama always said that when you want to make a good impression you should put your best foot forward. On the first day in a new school, Millie was determined to put her best foot forward.

She and Ruth put on the blue-and-white-flowered print dresses that Millie had made. Papa said they made the girls look like twins, especially since ten-year-old Ruth had taken a spurt of growing, while Millie seemed to be at a standstill. Millie couldn't quite agree with Papa, for her blond hair was so near white that she was called Cottontop, while Ruth's hair was a beautiful brown.

Ruth, too, was timid about starting a new school. She kept saying that it was too cold and that she might get sick going out barefoot. Her last year's shoes were too small too. Mama finally put a supporter waist on her to hold up her long stockings, then Ruth put on Millie's shoes.

When they were ready to go, Millie picked up the stack of sixth-grade books and said not a word. The girls looked into the face of the golden sun as they went down the road to school. Millie carried the half-gallon syrup bucket containing scrambled-egg sandwiches and squares of gingerbread. The frosty sand stung her bare feet and she shivered inside her old coat, now too small for her. But what made her really cold was her secret problem.

Huddling inside her coat, she said, "Ruth, I hope

Papa stays at this place at least long enough for us to finish this grade."

"So do I," Ruth said. "It's a lot easier walking a mile and a half down a straight road than four and a half miles over a mountain and across a foot log the way we did last year."

Millie clutched her books tighter as she and Ruth turned in at the schoolyard. A flying jenny and a see-saw on the playground were deserted. Some boys were playing catch on the sunny side of the grounds, and a group of girls chatted and giggled near the corner of the schoolhouse. Suddenly they grew quiet and stared at Millie and Ruth. As Millie started up the steps, the door opened and a middle-aged woman put out her arm and rang a hand bell. Millie squinted and pulled her neck in.

Children poured out of the schoolyard and pushed and shoved to get near the head of the line. But since Millie had been at the steps when the bell rang, she was first in line. Ruth was right behind her.

"Straight! Straight!" the teacher said, pointing with a stiff arm. "Boys, boys, stop that pushing."

Without looking back, Millie knew the line was forming straight out toward the road, and she doubted that a single child leaned this way or that. She wondered if the teacher could hear her heart pounding. Standing rigid, Millie studied the worn

steps made of used railroad crossties, and the doorsill, worn below the nailheads by the many feet that had passed over it.

As the line continued to form, Millie let her eyes travel slowly upward. The teacher's high-buttoned black shoes were badly worn, and her black poplin skirt was frayed at the hemline. Millie's eyes crept on up. The woman's long-sleeved, high-collared white blouse was starched and ironed to perfection, and her black hair was drawn back smooth and tight.

"You may pass in now," the teacher said, stepping to one side.

Millie went up the steps and inside the door, but then she hesitated, not knowing which way to turn.

"Move on," the teacher said, giving Millie a little push.

The sudden jangling of the hand bell had startled Millie, and now the teacher's little push added to her nervousness. Quickly she shifted the dinner bucket, reached back for Ruth's hand and marched straight to the teacher's desk, where they waited stiff and still while the other children took their seats.

There was an empty double desk near the front, and the teacher told Millie and Ruth to put their books there and then hang their coats on a nail on a side wall. When the girls returned, the teacher had her roll book out.

"I am Miss Comstock," she said. "Are you twins?"

"Oh, no, ma'am," Millie said.

"All right, what are your names and ages and what grades are you in? I'll take the younger first."

"My name is Ruth Holliway and I'm ten years old and I'm in the third grade." Ruth spoke barely above a whisper.

Millie was surprised but proud that Ruth had said "third grade."

"Well, I can hear you when you're standing this close," Miss Comstock said, "but when you recite in class you'll have to talk louder than that."

Miss Comstock looked at Millie. "And you?"

When Millie gave her name, age, and grade, Miss Comstock frowned slightly and said, "Are you sure you can do sixth-grade work?"

Millie thought the teacher must be reading her mind as plain as she would read spelling words on a blackboard. She gulped and managed to say, "No, ma'am, but I'd like to try." If only she could think of something quickly to make Miss Comstock believe she could do things. She looked at her hands.

"I can do lots of things," she blurted out. "I made my dress, and Ruth's too."

"Oh, a bright one in our midst." Miss Comstock smiled. "Not only are you smart, but you can sew, and I suppose you can bake a cherry pie, too."

Millie couldn't speak. Was the teacher laughing at her? Miss Comstock continued, "Well, honey, we don't favor little smarties here, and we don't have any teacher's pets."

A wave of giggles swept the room. Millie's face burned and tears stung her eyes. If only she could turn to a tiny bug, she thought, and crawl through that crack at her bare toes.

Miss Comstock was saying, "Well, you two can't sit together, since there's so much difference in your grades. You, Millie, may sit over there."

Feeling her chin tremble, Millie picked up her books and went to the seat Miss Comstock had indicated in the outside row. She thought every pair of eyes in the room must be on her. And to make it worse, the bright morning sun shone full across her desk. She would have preferred being under a seat in some dark corner to sitting here in bright sunlight. Soon, however, she was thankful for the sun—at least it was warm and kind.

Miss Comstock assigned Ruth to a double desk with another third-grade girl, and Millie felt the teacher treated Ruth the same as the other children.

But Millie didn't get the same treatment, or so it seemed. During every sixth-grade class she held up her hand to answer questions, but Miss Comstock ignored her. The only time she was called on to recite was during spelling, the last class in the afternoon. The sixth, seventh, and eighth grades had the same spelling class. There were seven sixth-graders, four seventh-graders, and four eighth-graders. The children formed a line across the front of the room, and Miss Comstock read out the words. Only two eighth-grade girls were left standing when Millie misspelled the word Constantinople. Shaken and somewhat bewildered, she went to her seat. She had felt so sure of herself.

When school was out, Jane Rossman, an eighth-grade girl who wore a pink ribbon on the single braid of her soft brown hair, put her arm around Millie and said, "Don't you feel bad. It wasn't your fault that you missed that word. I think Miss Comstock mispronounced it just to see if you'd miss it."

Millie stared in disbelief at the older girl.

"But—but Jane," Millie stammered, "I don't think the teacher would do that."

"Well, I do," Jane insisted, her blue eyes narrowing. "She pronounced it Con-stan-*tan*-ople instead of Con-stan-*tin*-ople, and that's what caused you to miss it."

"You better watch your step, gal," a barefoot, ragged-haired boy said as he brushed past Millie. "Ole lady Cornstalk don't like smart alecks, and she's got her claws out for you."

Millie winced. The boy ran wildly down the road,

whamming the smaller children with his tattered coat as he went.

Looking for Ruth, Millie saw her arm in arm with her seatmate. The weather had turned warm during the day, and Ruth had taken off Millie's shoes and was carrying them as she skipped along the sandy road. Apparently Ruth was going to make it fine, which was a relief to Millie. It looked as if she would have enough troubles of her own.

"Now, Millie, don't you let things get you," Jane said as she left the road to cut across a cornfield.

Other children dropped out along the way to take a trail through the woods or across a field. Soon only Millie and Ruth and two children living south of their house remained. Millie meant to make Ruth promise not to say anything to the family about her trouble with the teacher, but Ruth seemed so happy that Millie decided she hadn't noticed there was any trouble. She didn't mention it to Ruth.

The delicious, spicy smell of molasses cookies met them at the front door. Ruth threw her books on the standtable in the front room and hurried to the kitchen. Millie followed, only a little slower.

"Oh, Mama, those smell good." Ruth exclaimed.

"Go change your school dresses first," Mama said.

After the girls had changed and hung up their school dresses they went back to the kitchen and helped themselves to the cookies.

"How was school?" Mama asked, pouring two glasses of milk.

"Oh, fine," Ruth said around a mouthful of cookie. "And you know what? Our teacher's name is Miss Comstock, and some of the kids call her Miss Cornstalk."

Mama nearly spilled the milk. "Well, don't you ever call her that. Do you hear me?"

"Yes, ma'am." Ruth bowed her head.

"You remember always to do as you would be done by," Mama said, still looking at Ruth. "You wouldn't want others to make light of your name, so don't you ever make light of anybody else's name."

Millie drank her milk, took a handful of cookies, and went quietly out the door. She tossed half a cookie to Blue, where he lay under the clothesline, and went out the gate. Trixie followed as Millie wandered aimlessly through the thick undergrowth of brush that began just past the back-yard fence.

Some distance behind the house she found a ledge of rock jutting out of the hillside. She stepped out on it and looked around. A wide, shallow draw in the pasture land began here, and to the north was a pond. Beyond the pond lay a field, brown and bare, and beyond the field was a line of trees in fall colors of yellows, reds, and browns. The trees grew along the banks of Muddy Boggy Creek, which flowed through the low, rounded hills.

The timber was heavy here and Millie couldn't see very far in some directions, but apparently the chain of hills continued in a semicircle banding the north, the west, and the south. The Holliway farm was in a valley that fanned out toward the east and included other farms and the schoolhouse. About a mile north of the schoolhouse the creek flowed eastward; the

Holliways had forded it the day they moved here. From her ledge of rock, Millie looked back at the barn with its long sheds on either side. At that moment a flock of pigeons wheeled up from the barnyard and alighted in a line along the ridgepole.

Millie saw these things, but her mind was on school and the teacher she had so hoped to please. Put your best foot forward, Mama always said. Millie had tried so hard to do just that, and yet it seemed she had gotten off on the wrong foot at every turn.

The Family Shares
a Burden

Millie sat down on the moss-covered rock and gave
Trixie a piece of cookie. "Are you as lonesome as I
am?" she asked the little black-and-white dog. How
had she gotten off on the wrong foot with her teacher
today? She had always had the highest respect for
schoolteachers, feeling that they were among the
greatest people in the world. She thought about what
the ragged-haired boy had said.

"I don't believe it," she told Trixie. "I just don't
believe a schoolteacher would treat anybody like
that. How could she?" But Millie couldn't deny that
Miss Comstock had seemed to ignore her all day, had
deliberately looked right around her raised hand to
call on other children to answer. And there was Jane
Rossman's remark about the misspelled word. No
matter how hard Millie thought about it, nothing
seemed to make any sense.

"Maybe if I'd stayed in the fifth grade none of this would have happened."

For answer, Trixie licked her hand.

"But you can't get anywhere by staying in the same grade," Millie declared.

Trixie's tongue shot out and brushed Millie's cheek.

"All right, come on. I'll race you back to the house."

The family settled around the fireplace after supper. Mama took up her rugwork and Papa adjusted the kerosene lamp and began reading his *Farmer-Stockman* newspaper. Millie dreaded starting her homework, for she knew everyone would find out what she had done. Charles, who wanted very much to be in school, eagerly asked, "Millie, how far over in the books is the fifth grade?"

Millie shrank in her chair. "I don't know. I started in the sixth."

Charles's blue eyes grew wide with surprise. Mama stopped her work and exclaimed, "Dear me, child. After going in the fifth only a few weeks last winter? What if you can't make it? Then you'll have to suffer the embarrassment of being put back in a lower grade."

"Of course she can make it," Papa said over the top of his newspaper. "A body can do anything he sets his mind to—if he believes in it and is willing to work hard enough."

Millie drew in a great gulp of air and ran to her papa and threw her arms around his neck. There it was, all out in the open. What a relief to know that her family shared her burden. Millie believed in what she was doing and she wasn't afraid of hard work, so maybe with the help of her family she could make it. Charles helped Millie with her homework, and then they helped Ruth. Theron didn't take much interest in what they were doing; he had said last spring that he was through with school.

But, unfortunately, things didn't seem to improve at school. It was as plain as the big freckle on the back of Buster Emerson's neck that Miss Comstock avoided asking Millie questions during class periods. If the teacher wouldn't let her recite, would she lower her grades? Millie would have liked to talk the whole thing over with her family, but the only thing she could say for sure was that she didn't think Miss Comstock liked her. And wouldn't that sound silly! As if she wanted to be teacher's pet. No, she decided, this was one problem she'd have to work out by herself.

If only Miss May would come, she thought one night as she tossed in bed. Miss May lived alone in Atoka, about eight miles away, and Millie had known her all her life. Just about every winter, Miss May came to stay awhile with the Holliways. Lying there in the darkness, Millie thought of the little white-

haired lady with the crippled hands. She loved Miss
May's hands; they were kind and gentle, and they
could sew and knit and quilt almost as fast as anybody's. Miss May made lovely things, some to give
away and some to sell, and she had helped Millie
with her schoolwork more than any other one person.
But again, what could Millie say, even to Miss May?
She turned and tossed and finally slept.

One evening as they shelled corn for the fowls,
Millie said, "Charles, can a teacher fail a person just
because she doesn't like them?"

"Well, I reckon she could," Charles answered.
"Why?"

"Oh, I just wondered. Seems like Miss Comstock
doesn't like some of the children too well."

Charles held out a handful of corn to a long-necked
turkey gobbler. "It's impossible for a teacher to
like *all* kids."

Millie bit her lower lip.

"Theron and I went hunting this morning and we
saw where your schoolteacher lives," Charles said.

"Oh? Where?"

"In a little house with a picket fence around it
over on the first section line south of the schoolhouse," Charles explained. "We met a grown boy in
the woods over there. His name is Bob Rossman and
he said his sister Jane goes to school."

"Yes, I know Jane," Millie interrupted. "She's real nice."

"Bob said the schoolteacher and her mother live alone, and that the mother is sick a lot of the time," Charles continued.

Wrinkling her forehead in deep thought, Millie threw a handful of shelled corn and the white ducks squalled loudly, *quack, quack, quack!*

"Oh, yes," Papa said to the ducks as he came by with a bucketful of feed for the hogs, "you holler *half! half! half!* till you get there, then you take it all."

Millie followed Papa to the hog pen, climbed up on the rail fence and watched the hogs eat.

"They're looking real good, Cottontop," Papa said. "Soon as it gets cold enough we'll butcher."

Millie Takes Over

When the family was sitting around the fire that night, Papa said, "Sarah, do you want to go to town with me tomorrow?"

Mama let the rugwork fall in her lap. "Well, I'd like to, but I wish you'd mentioned it sooner. I've already set a batch of light bread to rise."

"Seemed like I couldn't make up my mind," Papa said. "There's so much to do about the place before bad weather sets in that the boys and I need to do all we can every day. Then I got to thinking about the girls needing shoes for school. I allowed you might like to go in and pick them out, and maybe visit May while you're in town."

Millie jumped up. How she would like to go to town herself. Not only to pick out her own shoes, but also to see Miss May. She waited for Papa to suggest that they all go.

"I don't know," Mama was saying. "I'd like to go, but if I do, that whole batch of bread will spoil."

"Oh, Mama, go on," Millie urged, hoping Mama would bring Miss May back. "I can manage the bread."

"Now there's a daughter for you," Papa said.

Mama looked at Millie. "Do you really think you could?"

"Sure, Mama," Millie said. "You already have everything in it that goes in. All I'll have to do is knead it and make it into loaves."

Talk of town and what they needed to buy and the possibility that Miss May woud come home with them got Millie so excited, she couldn't study.

After washing their feet to go to bed, each girl put on a stocking and stood on a piece of paper while Mama marked all the way around her foot so she could get the right-size shoes. Right after breakfast the next morning, Mama explained to Millie how to knead the bread dough after two risings, how to cut and shape it into four loaves, and how to place them in the deep pan to rise again.

Millie kept saying, "Yes, Mama. Yes, Mama. I've watched you do it so many times."

Papa had gone to the barn to hitch Bob and Becky to the wagon, so Mama hurriedly dressed. She combed her rich chestnut-colored hair into a figure eight at the nape of her neck. Then she slipped into her white blouse with the long, ruffled sleeves and the high, ruffled collar and Millie buttoned the tiny pearl buttons down the back. Finally Mama eased her brown woolen skirt over her stacks of petticoats and buttoned the waistband. Pulling her brown shawl across her shoulders, Mama said, "I guess I'm ready."

"Mama, you look pretty enough for church," Millie said. "Be sure and bring Miss May home with you."

"Child, I can't bring her if she doesn't want to come," Mama said. "But I will ask her."

The girls went out on the front porch and watched Papa help Mama up into the spring seat. "Be good girls," Mama called. "And don't forget the bread."

"We will. I mean, I won't. I mean—don't worry." Millie shook her head at her stammering and went into the house.

The girls barely got the dishes washed and the beds made in time to cook dinner for Theron and Charles. Theron said Millie's corn bread was awful, but Charles said it tasted all right crumbled in milk. Right after dinner, the boys went back to their fall plowing.

Millie had kneaded the bread dough at ten o'clock, as Mama had said, and now she tackled it again at one o'clock. She had to stand on a box to be high enough to handle it. The ball of dough was so

big it had to be set in a dishpan to rise, and it was
so heavy that Millie could barely lift it to turn it out
onto the breadboard. As she folded the edges over
and pushed down, the dough stuck to her hands and
went nearly to her elbows.

"How Mama manages this stuff is more than I
know," she wailed. "It looks so easy when she does
it."

"I reckon she's gonna get you for making a mess
of her bread," Ruth commented.

Millie looked daggers at Ruth. She tried to round
the dough into one big ball, the way Mama did.
Then, taking a long butcher knife, she cut it in half.
Then she cut each piece in half again. She formed the
quarters into loaves and placed them side by side in
the deep bread pan and set them to rise for the last
time. Standing back and looking at the lopsided
loaves, she felt terrible. She had so hoped they'd turn
out all right.

She felt disappointed about the bread, but her biggest disappointment came when Mama and Papa
returned without Miss May.

"Why didn't she come, Mama?" Millie asked.

"She's doing some quilting and she couldn't afford
to leave her work," Mama explained. "But she
promised to spend Christmas with us."

"Oh, goody!" Millie said. And then—"Mama, I dread for you to see what a mess I've made of the bread."

"Child, what have you done?" Mama asked.

Millie shook her head. "I just don't know how you do it."

Mama went straight to the kitchen and looked at the bread. "Why, child, you scared me. I don't see anything wrong with it. Build up the fire while I change my dress. The bread is ready to bake."

To Millie's surprise, the loaves really had evened up quite a bit in rising. She hurried with the fire, for she could hear Ruth rattling the heavy wrapping paper on the packages Mama and Papa had bought. As soon as she had the fire going, she ran into the front room and Mama gave the girls their new shoes. They were black with high-button tops. Millie ran to the sewing-machine drawer and got the buttonhook.

First the girls pulled on new long stockings. Then they put on their shoes, after Mama put the boxes and lids on the floor for them to stand in so they wouldn't scar the soles, in case the shoes didn't fit.

Millie buttoned her shoes and stood up. "Mama, they feel too big."

"We have to get them too big to start with," Mama explained. "Otherwise you'd outgrow them before spring."

The girls squealed with delight when Mama unwrapped a big bundle and they saw two beautiful coats. Mama handed Millie the blue one and Ruth the green one. Millie grabbed hers and buried her face in the folds. They put the coats on and turned about for Mama to see. The sleeves came down over their hands and the skirts came to their shoe tops. But Mama would hem them up.

New Pets

One Sunday afternoon Papa announced that tomorrow he and the boys would start clearing new ground.

"We'll cut all the good wood and rick it. Then later we can haul it to town and sell it. We'll dig out and burn the stumps and brush, and we'll have more ground for planting."

When Papa and Theron and Charles worked in the woods they came across many small animals. One day Charles brought home a young raccoon and built a special cage for him. The children thought and thought about a name for the furry little animal. He had bright black eyes and white rings around his brownish-black tail.

Suddenly Millie said, "Charles, why don't we name him Rickey? Rickey Raccoon."

"Ah, that's neat," Charles said, pushing dry bread crusts through the wire. "Rickey Raccoon. I like that name."

At first Rickey wasn't the least bit friendly. But then Trixie and Blue were not friendly to him either; they barked uproariously and kept the raccoon scared half out of his wits. But soon the dogs decided Rickey belonged there. And when he learned that nobody was going to hurt him, Rickey began to grow into a charming pet. In no time at all he was riding on the children's shoulders and snooping in their pockets for bits of food.

Mama allowed Rickey to sleep on the warm hearth during the day, but he had to be taken back to his box at night. When he was left inside, as soon as the lights were out and the house was quiet he'd start pilfering. He'd pad softly to the kitchen and climb up on the table where he'd get into the sugar bowl or the leftovers. The children thought this was cute, but Mama didn't agree. After Rickey scattered hominy over the kitchen floor, she insisted that he be taken back out to his cage at bedtime.

One day Charles said to Millie, "I know where there's a hollow tree with a family of squirrels living in it. If you'll help me build a squirrel cage, I'll catch them and we'll have them for pets too."

Millie wasn't sure Charles knew what he was doing, but she held the boards while he sawed and hammered. Then she held the chicken wire in place while he nailed it to the wooden frame. When the cage was finished it was as high as her shoulder. Charles scratched his head and said, "I didn't aim to get it that big. But I guess it'll give them plenty of room to play."

Papa helped Charles build a scaffold under an oak tree in the back yard and they nailed the squirrel cage on it. This would keep any prowling dogs from trying to get the squirrels.

"Charles, how will you catch the squirrels?" Millie asked.

He winked at her and said, "I think I've got a way figured out. You come to the barn and help me." So at his instructions, she held the open end of a tow sack around a keg hoop while he sewed it in place with a sacking needle and twine.

Millie grinned. "Surely you don't think you're going to catch squirrels with this?"

"You wait and see." Charles's blue eyes sparkled.

Millie didn't have to wait long. When she and Ruth came home from school the next day they found three young squirrels in the cage. Charles had put a short length of hollow log filled with leaves in one corner. At first the squirrels hid in there most of the time, but in a few days they began to venture out of

the log when Charles or Millie put corn or nuts in
the cage. Eventually they began to creep up, snatch
a bit of food from the children's hands, and dart
to the far side of the cage to eat it.

The days and nights had grown very cold, and one
evening Millie and Ruth arrived home to find the
rest of the family down at the barn butchering hogs.
Mr. Rossman and Bob were helping, and when it
came time for them to go home Papa gave them a
nice fresh liver and a side of spareribs. And Papa said

that he and the boys would help the Rossmans with
their butchering the next week.

Millie stood under the shed and watched Papa cut
up the three dressed hogs into hams, middlings,
spareribs, and other pieces. Then Theron and Charles
carried the meat up the ladder and laid it out to
cool overnight on the roof.

The next day, Friday, Millie and Ruth stayed
home from school to help with the work. The boys
brought the pieces of meat down from the roof and
Papa stacked them in layers in a big box in the smokehouse, putting lots of salt between each layer. Then
Papa built a fire under the black wash pot and began
rendering the small pieces of fat meat into lard.

Mama cut some flour sacks into wide strips and
Millie sat at the sewing machine and stitched them
into long, slender bags. The children took turns at
grinding a tubful of lean meat for sausages. The
grinder was clamped onto the edge of the table and
Millie turned it till her arm was sore and her hand
was blistered.

Every now and then, Mama sprinkled salt, crushed
red peppers, and crushed sage leaves over the
ground meat. When the last piece of meat was
ground, Mama mixed it with her hands. Then she
patted out little sausages, fried them golden brown,
and gave each child a sample.

"Oh, Mama, they're just right," Millie said. "Please don't put in any more pepper."

Millie took two sausages out to Papa, where he was stirring the lard in the wash pot. Papa chewed and tasted and smacked his lips. "They're good, but tell your mother to add more red pepper."

Millie winced and took the message to Mama. She watched apprehensively as Mama crushed two more long bright red pods of pepper and worked them into the meat. She could just see herself breaking her sausages apart and picking out the red flakes and the yellow pepper seeds. As Mama stuffed each long cloth bag with the sausage mixture she rolled it on the table to make it round. Then Charles took it out and hung it in the smokehouse.

The weekend was so busy and exciting that Millie forgot about school. But when she got there Monday morning, Miss Comstock looked at her and asked, "Millie, why were you girls absent last Friday?"

"We stayed home to help with the butchering," Millie answered.

Miss Comstock smiled. "Are you sure you helped, or were you just in the way?" The teacher was shuffling through some papers on her desk and she didn't look up when she asked this last question. Millie thought, "She's laughing at me again." A lump came up in her throat and she turned and went outside and stood alone until the bell rang.

In the days that followed, Millie would often glance up and catch Miss Comstock looking at her. The teacher's dark eyes would be fixed in a stare, and her mouth would be drawn down in a thin line. Millie would look quickly away, thinking to herself, "She hates me. How she hates me!"

Supposing this to be her punishment, Millie kept asking herself, "Is it worth it?" And her answer would always be, "Yes, it is worth it. I want to finish all twelve grades someday and I'm not going to let a crosspatch ole teacher keep me from it." Then she'd scold herself for thinking ugly thoughts about a schoolteacher. Sometimes it was all she could do to put her problem out of her mind. She thought that with Charles's help she learned more at home than she did at school—but maybe it only seemed that way. One night while they were studying at the kitchen table, Charles said, "Sister, if I don't get started to school pretty soon you'll have to help me instead of me helping you."

Now that winter had come and the wild animals were growing heavy fur, the boys often called the dogs and went hunting after supper. Theron said he

wanted Blue to get as much training as possible before the season set in in earnest. Theron was sometimes pleased with the young dog's progress, and sometimes he was impatient with him.

Theron and Charles kept a trap line in the woods and every morning, right after breakfast, they made the rounds of their traps. By the middle of December they had one wall of the barn nearly covered with pelts, turned inside out and stretched on boards to dry. They would sell the hides or trade them to a storekeeper for things they wanted.

One night Papa announced that he and the boys had the clearing finished and that tomorrow they would start hauling the wood to Atoka to sell. So the boys took a lantern to the barn, took down all the dry pelts, and tied them into a bundle. There were wolf, raccoon, skunk, and opossum hides. Theron whistled low and said, "How much do you think we'll get for them, Charles?"

"Plenty, I hope," Charles answered.

Besides the wood and the pelts, there were two tow sacks full of pecans that the family had gathered, and several pounds of golden butter that Mama had churned and saved to sell. The next morning Papa and the boys left for town in the two wagons before Millie and Ruth left for school. That evening, the brothers were wearing handsome new hunting jackets. Millie rubbed her face against Charles's woolen plaid jacket. "Umm, this sure smells better than the skunk hides you traded for it."

Panther Stories

Light sleet pelted Millie and Ruth as they went to school. They hurried along, and when they got there they found Miss Comstock and some of the children huddled around the box heater in the middle of the room. The boys were talking about a panther they said was running wild down along Muddy Boggy.

"Now wait just a minute, boys," Miss Comstock said sternly. "You're not supposed to tell this thing if it isn't so."

"Oh, it's so, all right," Willie Ketcherside declared. "Pa went hunting in the rain yesterday, and he heard it scream, and he saw its tracks down in our bottom field."

Miss Comstock looked at Willie. "If your father didn't actually see the animal, how does he know it was a panther? How does he know the tracks were not just big dog tracks?"

56

Willie stuffed his hands in his pockets and kicked the stove leg with the toe of his ragged boot. "Pa knows what a dog track looks like," he said hotly.

Miss Comstock rubbed her arms. The children looked at each other, and then they all began talking at once. Many of them had to go through thick woods to get to and from school, and Millie knew how scared they must be. But in spite of Miss Comstock's efforts to change the subject, the children talked about the panther.

It was still sleeting when school was out that afternoon, and Millie hoped the teacher wouldn't make them stand outside in line. But five minutes before time to go, Miss Comstock gave the signal. The children began sorting out the books they'd take home, and putting the others in their desks. Quietly and orderly, the children put on their wraps and returned to their seats.

"You may rise," Miss Comstock said. Everyone rose and stood by his desk. "Turn." They turned. "Pass." One aisle at a time, beginning with the higher grades, the children filed out. Since Millie was in the first row, she was out at the gate when the last child stepped down off the slippery steps.

"Turn," Miss Comstock said. All the children turned and faced her. "Dismissed." The teacher waved. The children let out wild whoops and scattered in all directions.

The storm was blowing from the northwest and Millie and Ruth pulled their toboggan caps low and hunched sideways to keep the sleet from stinging their faces. They had two very good reasons for going home faster than usual: the weather and the panther scare.

Ruth had told Mama the panther story before she had gotten her coat and cap off.

"Oh, come now," Mama said.

"That's what the boy said, Mama," Ruth declared.

"Now, look, Ruth," Mama said, "we can't believe everything we hear, and we can't go round telling everything we hear."

Just the same, when Papa and the boys came in to wash for supper they were told the story. Theron and Charles listened wide-eyed, but Papa said, "Well, every now and then a tale about a panther or a man-killer bear gets out." He reached for a towel and began drying his face. "I don't put much stock in such tales."

"I don't know, Papa," Theron said, pouring himself a pan of warm wash water. "There are places along Boggy where the woods are thick enough to hide a panther. It looks to me like one could be out there."

"Oh, it's possible." Papa stooped so he could see to comb his hair and mustache in the little square mirror over the wash bench. "But just saying one is out there doesn't make it so." He put the comb back in the crocheted comb pocket hanging on the wall. "Of course," he admitted, "if there is a panther out there, saying there isn't doesn't make it so either."

At the table, the children wanted to talk about the panther, but Papa talked of next year's crops.

Around the heater in the schoolroom, the panther tale grew. Nearly every morning a different boy vowed his father had heard or seen traces of the animal. No boy wanted to be left out of the adventure. To hear them tell it, the animal was black and slinky, had yellow eyes and a red mouth and a long, twitchy tail. One night Millie had a terrifying dream that the panther was on her back. Apparently Ruth was having the same dream, for both girls jumped up in the middle of the bed screaming at the same time.

"What on earth, girls!" Mama cried, coming with a lighted lamp.

"The panther!" Ruth screamed.

Mama shook Ruth to waken her. "Ruthie, there isn't any panther."

"He's in the bed!" Ruth screamed, clinging to Mama. "He's in the bed!"

"Look, baby," Mama said, "I'll turn the covers all the way back and show you there's not any panther."

With one big sweep, Mama threw the covers down over the foot of the bed. Then she and the girls screamed again. Papa and Theron and Charles came

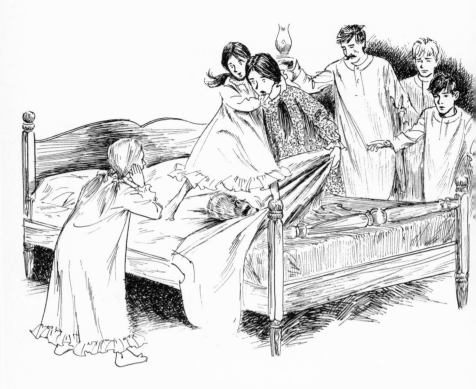

running in their nightshirts. The whole family stood staring at a rolled-up ball of black fur. Charles had forgotten to take him out, and Rickey Raccoon had gotten into bed with the girls.

Millie rubbed her shoulder. "Whooh, that scared me. I guess that pesky coon was what I felt on my back."

"That's what I felt on my face, too," Ruth said crossly. "Only I dreamed it was the panther." She begged Mama to leave the lamp burning low, and Millie had to admit that she felt better in a lighted room.

Attendance at school dropped to about half, and Millie wondered if it was caused by the bad weather or by the panther scare.

One evening when the girls got home from school they let out wild cries of delight. There by the fireplace sat Miss May. Mama and Papa had been to town and had brought Christmas company home with them. Millie was so happy she forgot to hang up her new coat or change her school dress or eat an after-school snack. She had to tell Miss May all about school—all, that is, except her trouble with the teacher. She couldn't, she absolutely would not tell Miss May her trouble. She would tell only the good part.

Miss May was a good listener. Millie showed her how far she was in the schoolbooks and showed her all of her written work.

"Hmm," Miss May said, shuffling the papers. "You've made some mighty good grades here. Although I wouldn't have advised it, I'm proud of you for tackling the sixth. After all, a body ought to do the best he can."

"If I keep making grades like these do you think I'll pass?" Millie asked.

"Why, you can't fail."

Millie wanted to say, "Even if the teacher hates me?" but she didn't.

That night Papa was restless. Eventually he said, "Children, I hate to add anything to the story that's going around . . ."

The children looked at him and waited.

Papa stirred the fire and put the poker back in its place. "In town today, a man living way back here in the bend of Boggy said one of his cows had been killed out in the woods and most of it had been eaten by some wild animal when he found it."

The children's eyes grew round, and Millie felt her skin prickle.

"Of course, the man insisted that the panther did it," Papa continued. "I questioned him about it, and he admitted that it all happened in a spot where the leaves were deep and where there were no tracks that he could be absolutely sure about. I pointed out that the cow could have been accidentally shot by hunters and that wolves and other animals could have eaten the carcass."

Millie moistened her lips and swallowed hard.

"I just wanted to tell you boys so you'd be careful when you're out hunting," Papa said. "All we can do when one of these tales gets out is to keep a keen eye and a cool head. Chances are, it'll all blow over by spring and we won't hear any more about it."

Everyone was silent for quite some time. Then a smile gradually crept over Miss May's face and she asked, "Have you children ever heard your father's panther story?"

Papa's head shot up off the pillow on the back of his chair. He grinned at Miss May, then leaned back again.

"Tell us, Papa," the children urged.

"Let May tell it," Papa said. "She's the one that recollected it."

The children looked at Miss May, but she said, "I wasn't there."

"Tell us, Papa," the children begged.

With his brown mustache slightly spread in a grin, Papa looked at Miss May as if to say, "Why didn't you keep quiet?" But presently he cleared his throat and began.

"Well, once upon a time—I reckon that's the way a good story starts—there was this young couple who had a tiny baby. It was their first one and they were so proud of him that the mother thought she just had to take him and show him off to his grandmother. That would be her mother."

The children nodded.

"Well, early one morning the father put the side-saddle on his wife's horse and led him up to the front door."

"What is a sidesaddle, Papa?" Ruth asked.

"A sidesaddle? Why, it's a saddle with one stir-rup," Papa explained. "Sidesaddles were for women only. It used to be that a woman was considered in-decent if she rode astraddle of a horse. Truth is, I don't see how she stayed on."

"Yes, but what about the panther?" Theron asked.

"Well, it was winter, like now," Papa continued, "so the young woman wrapped her little baby in lots of quilts to keep him warm. Her husband helped her up into the sidesaddle, then he handed up the baby. I imagine he said something like 'You be careful now, and be sure and be home before dark.' And she likely promised to do just that. But it was a long way through awfully thick woods, and when she got there, the two women were so happy visiting and fussing over the little baby that they forgot all about the time and the young woman stayed too late. Suddenly she jumped up to go, but the sun went down before she got very far.

"The trees were thick and overlapped, so it was nearly dark on the road. The young mother held her baby tight to her breast as she slapped the horse with the reins. Suddenly she heard a scream, loud and terrifying like a woman in great danger. But it wasn't a woman, it was a panther, and she knew it. And the horse knew it, too, and he snorted and broke into a run, nearly upsetting the woman and her baby.

"Again the scream tore through the woods. It made cold chills run through the woman, and it made the horse run as fast as he could. The screams got louder and wilder, and the woman and the horse knew the panther was coming closer.

"The woman held her little baby tight and clung for dear life to the saddle horn. She didn't have to urge the horse to go faster. The panther was jumping from one treetop to the next, taking all the short cuts, and soon he would catch up with them. The woman's hand was getting tired on the saddle horn and her foot in the single stirrup felt as though it was about to break."

The children leaned forward in their chairs. Mama

was slowly braiding her rug, but Miss May's knitting was heaped in her lap.

"Back at home," Papa continued, "the young man got uneasy because his wife hadn't come. So he took his shotgun and jumped on his horse and went to find her. He had just reached the deep woods when he heard the panther scream. I imagine his hair stood on end. Well, anyhow, his horse whinnied and reared up and tried to run back. It didn't want to go near that panther. So the man had to dig the horse hard with his steel spurs to make it go on. Suddenly the horse stopped and reared up and wouldn't go another step."

"Yes?" Theron said.

"The man heard the hoofbeats of another horse coming toward him. In the dim light he saw it was his wife's horse, but she was lying so low in the saddle that at first he didn't see her. The horse passed him like a streak and he saw that his wife was still on, but he couldn't tell if she still had the baby. He looked up in time to see the panther against the sky. His horse was having such a fit that he jumped off and let it run back toward home.

"The man raised his gun and took careful aim. He knew he had to kill the panther with the first shot, for his shotgun was a single-barrel and he knew he wouldn't have time to reload if he missed.

"So he aimed very carefully," Papa repeated. "As the panther balanced on a big limb to spring down on him, BANG! went the gun. And the panther tumbled down in a heap."

"Whooh," Ruth sighed and fell back in her chair.

"What happened to the woman and the little baby?" Milly asked.

"Well, they were both sick for days and days," Papa said. "Everybody thought the baby was going to die from the awful hard bouncing he got. But I guess he was a tough little scrapper."

Smiling, Miss May said, "He's still tough."

The children looked from Papa to Miss May and back at Papa. "Who was the baby, Papa?" Millie asked.

Papa's blue eyes twinkled. "Well, Cottontop, I was."

"*You!*" the children gasped.

"See what I mean?" Miss May said. "He's still tough."

They all had a good laugh about that.

When Millie was ready for bed, she went to the kitchen to get a drink of water. Theron and Charles were already in bed. She heard them talking behind the curtain.

"You know, Charles, if a panther is out there in the woods I sort of hope we meet him," Theron was saying. "I believe I can kill him with Papa's double-barreled shotgun."

"I don't know." There was a chuckle in Charles's voice. "I think I'd come nearer strangling him to death with heel dust."

Millie ran and crawled into bed beside Ruth. She was glad Miss May's bed was in the same room with theirs. The girls snuggled close to each other. "Sister, what if that panther had got Papa when he was a little baby?" Ruth asked.

"Well, if he had we wouldn't be here, I guess."

Some minutes later, when Millie was nearly asleep, Ruth said, "I wonder what the world would be like without us."

"Hmm," Millie mumbled. "I really don't know."

On the last day of school before Christmas, the girls took all their books home. You could tell by the way Ruth put hers down that she didn't intend to pick them up again until it was time to go back to school. But Millie carefully stacked hers on the lower part of the standtable in the front room.

Mama and Miss May were baking, and the house was filled with delightful Christmas smells.

"Mama, since we have a chimney for Santa Claus to come down, can't we hang up stockings this year?" Millie asked.

"It sounds like a nice idea," Mama said.

"We want a tree, too," Ruth insisted.

"I thought we'd want a tree," said Charles, who was sitting behind the cookstove, picking out nuts, "so I've already cut one and put a stand on it."

"Good for you, Charles," Mama said. "We can put it between the fireplace and the front door."

"Whatever I do to help decorate it I want to do tonight," Charles said. "Tomorrow Theron and I are going hunting all day."

"Hunt all day on Christmas Eve?" Millie said. "I guess if that's what you want to do, it's all right. But not me. I want to stay in the house and help with the baking."

"Naturally," Charles said. "That's what women like. But hunting is a man's pleasure."

Counting Miss May's, there would be seven stockings to hang up. Millie brought in the nails and the claw hammer and laid them on the mantel. After supper Mama popped the corn, then the family strung long strings of it and wound them around the tree. And they made popcorn balls and hung them on the branches. It was a beautiful fat Christmas tree, all green and white with a silver star on the top. Whatever gifts Santa couldn't put in the stockings he could leave under the tree.

The Boys Go Hunting

Millie stood on the back porch and watched her
brothers and the dogs go down past the barn and out
of sight. It was a cold, damp morning, and she
wished they'd stay home. Papa came out to draw a
bucket of water and Millie said, "Papa, could Theron
kill a panther with your shotgun?"

Papa's hands rested on the well rope above his
head, and he looked down at her a long moment before replying. "Yes, if he hit the right spot. But don't
you go worrying yourself all day about the boys. I
doubt that there's a panther out there."

Millie went in and stood behind the warm cookstove. She wanted to believe as Papa did about the
panther, but just believing a thing didn't make it so.
Papa had said that. She had to do something to keep
her mind busy. Coming from behind the stove, she
said, "Mama, let me beat the eggs for the next cake."

"I'd be glad to," Mama said. So Millie pitched in and helped with the Christmas baking, trying hard to put any thought of the panther out of her mind.

Just before noon Ruth came into the kitchen carrying Rickey. "Mama, what do you want for Christmas?" she asked.

"Well, let's see." Mama was icing a cake. "If I made out a list, the first thing would be health and happiness for my family. And the next thing would be plenty of food and clothing and a good house to live in. But since we have all those things there's no need to wish for them, is there?" Mama smiled at Ruth. "You know, child, maybe instead of wishing for more, I ought to just take time to be thankful for what I have." She finished the cake and set it up on a shelf. "What do you want for Christmas, Ruth?"

"Wel-l-l," Ruth said slowly, pulling Rickey away from her face, "I don't need to wish for pets. Because counting the three squirrels and Trixie and Blue and this coon and all the cats down at the barn, we have plenty of pets."

"I agree with you there," Mama said.

"And I don't need to wish for a doll," Ruth continued, "because Millie and I have beautiful dolls. What do you want, Millie?"

"Right now," Millie said, vigorously scrubbing a mixing bowl, "I wish Charles and Theron would come home."

"So do I," Mama said. "That mist is heavy out there, and I wish they'd come in out of it."

"Looks like you'll get your wish," Miss May said. "Here come the dogs now."

"Well, good," Millie said. "I guess the boys stopped at the barn to skin a skunk or something."

"Well, if it's a skunk I hope they stay at the barn to skin it," Miss May said, laughing. "And I hope they practically skin themselves before they come in."

"That's why I didn't want them to go hunting," Millie declared. "Every time they catch a skunk they come in with that awful ole stink on their clothes. I didn't want the house to be stunk with skunk on Christmas." She bit her lower lip. Why had she said that? She hadn't even thought of it till this instant. But just thinking that her brothers were safe was such a relief that she didn't want anyone to know how worried she had been.

But the boys didn't come to the house. And when Papa went to the barn to call them to dinner they were not there.

"It is strange that the dogs came in without them," Papa admitted as they sat down to the table. "But then you can't depend on a dog as young as Blue."

Everyone glanced at everyone else and then Millie looked down at her plate. Suddenly she wasn't hungry. "I guess I licked too much cake batter and ate too many nuts," she said lamely.

"You'd better eat," Mama said. "At least a glass of milk and bread. That isn't sweet, and it might keep you from getting sick to your stomach."

After dinner they continued with the baking. But they talked less, and the happy excitement was missing. Millie kept going to the window and looking out. It was late afternoon when she looked out and cried, "The panther's got Charles!"

"What?" Mama dropped an egg on the floor.

"Oh, Mama, I'm sorry," Millie said. "I didn't mean to say that. But why is Theron by himself? And why is he running?"

Papa heard the commotion and came in from the front room. "Now, don't get excited," he said. "Wait till Theron gets here and we'll hear what's the matter." He opened the back door and waited for Theron, who was galloping up the slope.

Miss May grabbed a rag, gathered up the broken egg, and dropped it in the stove. She came to the door just as the gate banged behind Theron.

"Charles is lost!" Theron gasped.

Hands went over mouths and eyes opened wide. Theron practically fell inside and Papa closed the door.

"Let's keep calm now," Papa said, his voice trembling. "Come over by the fire, son, and tell us what happened." Millie pushed a chair under Theron, and he fell on it.

"We followed the trap line, just as usual. Then we decided to go a little farther. We crawled through our back fence and went on through the woods, that way." Theron pointed northwest.

"The woods were awful thick and we came to a creek and crossed it and I guess that's where Charles got turned around. That must be where we lost the dogs, too. I guess they didn't cross the creek with us." He paused for breath.

"We crossed on a tree where the bank had caved

off and the tree had fallen across the creek. Some of the roots were still in the bank and we picked our way through the limbs. I didn't think about the dogs at the time, then when I did think about them and called them, they didn't come. When I realized the dogs had left us, I said, 'Charles, let's go home.' He said, 'I'm ready. I'm about to freeze anyhow.' "

Mama put her hand over her mouth and Papa put his arm around Mama and said, "Go on, son."

"Well, I turned and started back this way, but Charles wanted to go the other way. I said, 'No, we go this way.' But he said, 'No, we go this way.' He said, 'I know we go this way because we crossed Boggy, and right over there is Boggy.' I said 'No, Charles, we didn't cross Boggy. We crossed a creek running into Boggy, but we didn't cross Boggy.' "

Theron shook his head and wiped his eyes. "He kept saying if he could just cross Boggy he knew he could find his way home. I don't know what made him think we crossed Boggy. I tried to reason with him that a tree the size of the one we crossed on wouldn't reach across Boggy, at least not there. But he wouldn't listen."

"Don't hold it against him, son," Papa said. "Sometimes when a body loses his bearings he gets scared. And when that happens he sometimes loses his reasoning too."

Theron got up and turned his back to the stove.

"The country back there sure is rough—one hill right after another. It sure is easy to get turned around. I thought maybe I could get him to come back this way with me, so I went on with him a little while longer. If it hadn't been so cloudy and misty I could have showed him the sun and maybe he would have got straightened out. But we couldn't even tell where the sun was supposed to be. He kept going farther and farther in the wrong direction. And when he started up this hill where I knew we hadn't been before, I got scared. I was afraid I'd get lost, too, then we sure would be in a fix.

"Finally I told him I wasn't going any farther. I kept hoping he'd turn back and follow me, but he didn't—he was so turned around and so dead sure we'd come from the other way. When I got about halfway up a hill coming this way, I looked back and caught a glimpse of him about halfway up a hill going the other way. I yelled and yelled, but he couldn't hear me. And that's when I started running home." Theron turned his back on the family and covered his face with his hands.

"You did the right thing, son," Papa said. "You come eat now, and I'll go look for Charles."

Theron wheeled around. "Papa, you don't understand! He's miles over yonder. You'll have to have a search party. You'll never find him by yourself."

Papa looked stunned. "All right," he choked. "All

right. You go eat. You'll need the strength. You'll have to lead the search party. While I get some men together, you put on dry clothes and eat a good meal."

Theron kept rubbing his legs; you could tell they ached from running so far.

Papa patted Mama's shoulder. "We'll find him, Sarah. Now you get Theron some dry clothes and give him plenty of good hot food. I'll go get some of the neighbor men and we'll find Charles."

Mama laid out some dry clothes for Theron, and he went behind the heavy curtain at the other end of the room to change. He stayed a long time, and Millie knew he was crying and didn't want anybody to see.

After a while Mama said, "Come on, son, and eat. Your Papa will be back with the men pretty soon and you'll need to get started." So Theron came and choked down some food. But he gave the dogs more than he ate.

Soon Papa came back with Mr. Dickson. Papa explained that Mr. Jones had gone to tell Mr. Rossman. "Jones said he and Rossman would go round this way on horseback," Papa motioned south and west, "and would meet us at the creek where the boys crossed this morning. He said he knew where that tree was."

Pointing with an outstretched arm, Mr. Dickson described the lay of the land. "Boggy flows this way for several miles, then it makes a big bend and comes right back this way about a mile south of us over on the other side of the hill."

South of the Holliway place, the land gradually rose to a hill. The Dicksons, the Joneses, and the Rossmans lived over in that direction.

"Right back here a few miles in this deep bend of Boggy is some of the roughest country you ever saw," Mr. Dickson continued. "There's one hill right after another, all covered with heavy timber. A body could get turned around in there easy and walk himself to death before he could find his way out."

"I don't think it will do any good for the men to meet us where we crossed the creek," Theron said. "Charles was determined to cross Boggy if he could, and he was following it, looking for a place to cross."

Mr. Dickson moved about restlessly. "There's an old swinging footbridge way back over there, that is if it hasn't already rotted and fallen in the creek. If the boy finds it and manages to cross the creek, we'll never find him tonight."

Millie held her breath. If Charles tried to cross on the bridge and it broke with him— She closed her eyes and refused to finish the thought.

"I can't think of any other place where the boy

could possibly cross Boggy, it being bank-full. . . ."
Mr. Dickson's voice trailed off.

Mama swayed and clutched at a chair back. Papa
steadied her and said, "Try not to worry too much,
Sarah. We'll find him. I'll take the dinner horn and
I'll blow it often, and if Charles hears it he'll
recognize it and he'll come to meet us."

Millie ran to the kitchen and got the small, yellow
cow horn for Papa. Theron had his and Charles's
hunting caps with the carbide lights on the bills.

"That's a good idea, Theron," Mr. Dickson said.
"Dark is bound to overtake us."

Papa picked up the shotgun and put a handful of
shells in his pocket. Mr. Dickson had his gun, too.
At the gate Theron looked back and said, "Mama,
keep Trixie and Blue here. They'd only get lost."

Mama called the dogs into the kitchen and closed
the door. Millie looked at Blue and said, "If Theron
hadn't traded Bulger for you maybe this wouldn't
have happened. You wouldn't know your way
around the barn and back." As she stared at the
young dog, he looked at her sorrowfully and crawled
under the cookstove.

Tears strained against Millie's eyelids, but she
tried to keep them back. Mama had enough grief
without anybody adding to it.

Charles Is Lost

"Come, Sarah," Miss May urged. "When Charles gets home he'll be happy to see that we went right on with the Christmas planning." But you could tell that Mama's heart wasn't in it. She just agreed to whatever Miss May suggested.

"Since the men will be hungry when they come in, why don't we bake a ham now?" Miss May asked, and Mama nodded.

Millie and Miss May went to the smokehouse and got one of the nicest hams. Then Miss May said, "Take the dishpan, girls, and run get me a pan of sweet potatoes to candy with the ham."

Millie and Ruth took a pan and started to the rick where they were stored. Shivering in the heavy mist, Millie thought Charles must be soaked through and through. Her chin quivered and she stumbled blindly over a rock.

"Sister, don't fall down," Ruth said.

Digging her way into the fodder, Millie filled the pan with potatoes, then she backed out, crawdad style, dragging the pan in front of her. She carefully covered the hole so the potatoes would not freeze or get wet. Then she and Ruth carried the pan between them to the house. Miss May was putting a pot of coffee to simmer on the back of the stove.

Millie went to the front room, but when she saw the green-and-white Christmas tree, hot tears began trickling down her cheeks. And there, sleeping peacefully on the warm hearth, was Charles's pet raccoon. Millie felt that she had to get out of the house.

Pulling on her old coat, she slipped quietly out the front door. Around the house she went, ducked under the fence, and ran as fast as she could to the ledge of rock at the head of the draw. The rock was wet, but she didn't want to sit down. She wanted to stand so she could see that much sooner if the men and Charles came over the rise.

It was cold. And lonesome, too. Papa had said that Charles could start school right after Christmas, and Millie had so looked forward to it.

Spot bawled down at the cow-lot gate, and Millie realized it was past time to do the chores. "At least I can feed the chickens," she told herself. At the house, she stuck her head in at the back door and said, "I'm

going to feed the chickens." If Ruth wanted to come
along she could, but Millie would just as soon she
didn't.

Sitting inside the barn out of the cold mist, Millie
shelled corn into a bucket. So many evenings she
and Charles had shucked and shelled the corn for
the poultry. Would they ever do it again? Millie's
eyes burned and she had to keep wiping her nose.
When she went out, and as she scattered feed about,

her eyes searched in all directions for the men and boys.

The brown turkey gobbled and the blue-and-white-speckled guinea hens potracked. The brood sow grunted, and Millie said, "Yes, I'll feed you too." She went back into the crib, got an armful of corn for the sow and threw it in the pen whole; the sow could bite off her own corn.

Mama and Ruth were coming with the milk buckets, and they were doing the same thing as Millie—looking and looking for Papa and the boys. Millie milked Pet while Mama milked Spot and Brownie. Then Millie filled the cats' bowl with warm milk. They fed the horses and started back to the house, still looking.

Millie stopped by the squirrel cage with some nuts and an ear of corn. The reddish-brown squirrels ran to meet her and flattened their bodies against the inside of the wire cage.

"I'm going in the house," Ruth said. "It's cold out here." She and Mama went inside.

Millie put her hand inside the cage and held it very still. The squirrels came up and gently touched her hand with their whiskers. Each took a single pecan, sat back on his haunches and began gnawing on it. Millie put the rest of the nuts down, closed the cage and turned toward the house.

The lamps were lighted and the warm kitchen smelled of baked ham, fresh light bread, and spicy sweets. Millie's stomach did a flip, and she slapped her hand over her mouth. She hadn't realized till now that she was terribly hungry. When Mama saw that she was about to be sick, she put her arm around her and said, "Charles will come home, Millie. Charles will come home." But Mama had to wipe her eyes on her apron.

"I'll bring in some firewood," Millie said. She had to stay out in the cold air until her stomach would behave. On her way to the woodpile she looked again, but there was no sign of Papa and the boys. By now it was so dark that she couldn't see past the barn. Could panthers see in the dark? They were of the cat family, so she guessed they could. She carried load after load of wet wood and piled it on the front porch. Then she carried a load into the house and put it on the fire. As she turned back to close the front door she looked toward the road, but it was so dark that she couldn't even see the gate.

"Now, child, hang up that wet coat and sit down and warm your feet," Miss May said. "We're all going to have something to eat."

Obediently Millie sat down on Mama's new braided rug and pointed her feet toward the fire. "Come here, you coon," she said, but she didn't need to—Rickey was already exploring her pockets. In spite of her grief and worry she smiled as the soft, furry animal reached into her dress pocket for the shelled corn she had brought him.

Ruth had gone to the kitchen with Miss May, and after a while they returned with a pitcher of hot chocolate, cups, and a plate of hot buttered bread. It tasted good, but no sooner had Millie eaten it than she had to jump up and run out on the porch and throw it up. She grabbed the gallery post and leaned way over. The others came out, and Mama held Millie's head.

"Oh, Mama," Ruth said, "there's not a star in sight, and it's as black out here as a panther."

Millie's stomach churned again, and Miss May said, "Ruthie, please don't talk like that."

They heard men's voices, and Millie cried, "Papa!" She would have run down the steps but Mama held her. They saw the carbide lights on the hunting caps as two men came around the corner of the house.

"Papa!" Millie cried again. "Is Charles with you?" Neither Papa nor Charles was with them.

"Oh, Theron, son, what happened?" Mama cried.

"We didn't find him, Mama," Theron answered. "Papa is still out there."

In the house, Theron and Mr. Dickson explained that Papa and Mr. Rossman had built a bonfire and that Papa would stay out all night. Mr. Jones had gone home, saying he'd warn other men to be ready to help with the search tomorrow. Mama turned very pale and clung to the chair.

"You try to keep hold of yourself, Miz Holliway," Mr. Dickson said awkwardly but kindly. "I thought I'd take some food and coffee back to the men."

"Yes, of course." Miss May turned toward the kitchen. "Millie?" she called.

"Yes, ma'am." Millie hurried after Miss May.

"Am I ever glad we baked this ham," Miss May said. Hurriedly she carved off thick tender slices and put them on a plate. Then she sliced a loaf of bread while Millie cut wedges of chocolate nut cake. Miss May wrapped the food in clean cloths and Millie brought a big milk bucket. First they put in a bowl of candied sweet potatoes, then the plate of ham, and on top of that the bread and cake.

"Cups and forks, Millie," Miss May said. Millie brought them quickly.

The big granite coffeepot had a bail as well as a handle. Mr. Dickson took it in one hand and the bucket of food in the other.

"I'll carry one," Theron said.

"No," Mr. Dickson spoke firmly. Then to Mama, "Put him to bed, ma'am. He's plumb tuckered out."

"Yes, I will," Mama promised, holding the back door open for Mr. Dickson.

"I'll go home from the woods tonight," he said from the back porch, "but I'll be back early in the morning. We'll find your boy."

Mama nodded and covered her face with her apron. Miss May eased the door out of her hand and closed it.

The fire in the fireplace was so hot that Rickey left the hearth in search of cooler quarters. Theron gently picked him up and took him out to his box.

While Theron ate supper, Mama filled two lanterns with kerosene and Millie polished the glass chimneys. They hung one lantern high in a tree in the front

yard and the other at the end of a long pole that
stuck out under the barn roof.

As they returned to the house from the barn,
Theron stopped and looked at the fuzzy spots of light
around both lanterns.

"Mama," he said, "in order to see those lanterns in
this fog Charles would have to come all the way
home."

"Yes," Mama answered sadly.

In the front room, Miss May joined the family as
they knelt in prayer.

"Our merciful, heavenly Father," Mama began,
"hallowed be Thy name in all the earth. Thou art
all powerful, and Thou knowest all things. If it be
Thy will, return our loved one to us unharmed." Her
voice trembled and she ended with, "Thou knowest
what is best, Father. Thy will, not ours, be done."

They lingered on their knees awhile longer, each
praying a silent prayer for Charles.

Later, as Millie lay face down across the foot of
Mama's and Papa's bed in the front room, she wondered about Mama's words "Thy will, not ours, be
done." She wanted to demand that God bring
Charles back to them *now*. But she knew it was wrong
to feel that way. Mama was right. God knew what
was best, and God didn't want harm to come to any
of His children. She whispered, "Please, dear God,
do keep him safe and bring him back to us."

A Strange Santa Claus

A rooster crowed and slowly Millie opened her eyes to a strange light. Where was she? She put out her hand and touched a face. Ruth sighed and pushed her hand away. Millie felt her clothing, then it all came to her. Someone had put her in her own bed, clothes and all. Only her shoes had been taken off. The dim light came from one of the lanterns. Slipping from under the warm covers, she stood shivering by the bedside. Miss May's bed at the other side of the room was smooth and untouched.

A thin line of yellow light showed under the door. Millie quietly opened the door. Miss May was standing by the window. Mama sat near the fire, gently rocking and staring at nothing. Millie ran over and stood by Mama. She didn't ask the agonizing question that screamed to be answered. She couldn't bear to make or to hear Mama say no.

The clock on the mantle struck, and Millie looked up. It was four-thirty in the morning.

"Put on your shoes, child," Mama said.

Millie saw the hammer and the seven nails she had put on the mantel. Oh, it seemed so long ago. Nobody had hung up the stockings last night, and this was Christmas morning. She buttoned her shoes and put the buttonhook back in its place.

"Mama, I'll build a fire in the cookstove so the kitchen will get warm," Millie said. Mama nodded.

When Millie had the fire going, she tiptoed to the other end of the room and peeped behind the cur-

tain. Theron was lying on his back, staring at the ceiling. She wondered if he had slept at all. Without looking in her direction, he put out his arm and she ran and fell across it. They clung to each other. His muscles twitched, and she knew he was crying inside.

"It wasn't your fault, Theron," she said, trying hard to control her voice.

Pushing her gently away, he said, "Run along so I can get up."

Back in the front room, Miss May poked at the fire. Millie said, "I'll bring in some wood." As she stooped over the wood she'd stacked on the porch last night, she heard footsteps in the yard.

"Papa?" she cried.

Rounding the corner of the house, Papa took one giant stride up on the end of the porch. Mama and Miss May ran out, and Mama cried, "Oh, John, you haven't found him?"

"No," Papa choked. He guided Mama back inside.

Theron stood white and questioning. Papa shook his head. "We haven't found a trace of him. But Mr. Rossman is still out there. I came to see if maybe . . ."

Millie ran back out and got the wood she'd been after, then Papa took it and put it on the fire.

"We kept a fire going all night," he explained.

"And we kept going out in wide circles, blowing the horn and firing the guns."

Mama fell in Papa's arms and sobbed. Millie and Miss May cried too. Ruth came running from her bed and stood shaking and crying in her flannel nightgown.

Papa stroked Mama's hair. "I don't know why it was," he said, more to himself than to others, "but about an hour ago I had a mighty strong feeling that the boy had found his way home."

Mama drew back, covered her mouth with her finger tips and stared at Papa. "John," she said hoarsely, "I had the same feeling. So strong it was that I went clear down past the barn and called to him."

Miss May shook her head and whispered, "Poor dears."

Papa spoke quickly, and there was a different tone in his voice. "Theron, let's go do the chores while the women get breakfast. We'll go back out there and look till we do find him."

Theron had been putting on his shoes as fast as he could. He grabbed his coat and cap off a nail and he and Papa took the milk buckets and hurried to the barn. They came back with the milk just as the women were putting breakfast on the table. Millie noticed that daylight was barely beginning to show.

Papa didn't mention Charles by name in the breakfast blessing, but he closed with "Thou knowest best, Father. Thy will be done."

Before anyone had time to butter the first biscuit, Trixie and Blue raced around the house, barking. Everyone left the table. Millie ran through the house and out the front door. In the dim morning light she saw two figures coming up the road. She supposed they were the first to come to start the new search party. Then the smaller one started running.

"Charles!" Millie screamed. "Charles, you've come home!" She ran to meet him. Suddenly they were in each other's arms, and Millie never could have told how they got in the house. Everyone cried and laughed and talked, and cried some more.

Millie looked up into the face of a strange man in ragged clothing standing near the Christmas tree. He was tall and thin, and there was a sad expression about his eyes. Millie ran and grabbed his hand. "You're a strange Santa Claus," she cried, "but you brought the only thing we wanted for Christmas." Then she dropped his hand and backed shyly away.

The dogs barked outside and Papa went to the door. Neighbors were coming to help take up the search again. "Come in, men," Papa called. "The boy is found. He's just come home." Two men hurried up the walk and stepped inside the house.

Folding and unfolding his ragged cap, the man who had brought Charles home tried to slip out. But Papa closed the door and said, "Don't go. We want to hear what happened. I don't believe I got your name."

"London. Josiah London," the stranger said.

"Well, Mr. London," Papa said, "this is Mr. Dickson, and this is Mr. Ketcherside." The men shook hands.

"Won't you sit down?" Papa motioned Mr. London to the best chair.

"No, thank you, sir," Mr. London said uneasily. He looked at Mama. "I—ah—I think the boy needs to eat, ma'am." There was a pained look on his face, as if he was trying to give Mama some secret message.

"Y-y-yes sir," Mama stammered. She and Miss May took Charles to the kitchen. Millie wanted to be with Charles, but she also wanted to hear what had happened. She stayed with the menfolks.

A Christmas to Remember

Millie trembled as she stood with Papa and Theron and Mr. Dickson and Mr. Ketcherside, waiting for the stranger to tell his story.

Shaking his head, Mr. London began, "The boy's taking it powerful hard. He ought not to have it throwed up to him."

"Of course not," Papa agreed. "But just where and how did you find him? And where do you live?"

Still twisting his cap, Mr. London nodded as if to say I'll answer all your questions, but I have to do it my way. "I'm new in these parts," he said. "Just moved in two days ago. Live in the first house north on the other side of the road."

Millie knew the place. It was only a shack, about two miles down the road.

"I went out yesterday to get me some game for

Christmas dinner," Mr. London continued. "I crossed the bridge to this side, but I kept close to the big creek—Boggy, I think you call it. I went on this-away" he motioned northwest—"till I came to a little creek flowing into the big one, and I crossed it."

Theron stepped up. "Did you cross on a tree with the limbs still on?"

"No," Mr. London said. "No, this was a big syca-more with all the limbs chopped off. You could tell it had been put there apurpose for a foot log."

Theron stepped back.

"Well," the man continued, "I went on quite a ways. I found a squirrel up in a tree so I brought him down with my rifle. And then I heard somebody yell, so I yelled back. 'I'm lost' the boy called, and I hol-lered back, 'Come thisaway, and keep hollering so we won't lose each other.' The woods is so thick back there that the owls hoot in the daytime."

"Go on," Papa coaxed.

"Well, we got to each other and the boy said he lived way over yonder, way on the other side of Boggy—he thought. It just goes to show how turned around he was. I followed him quite a ways along the bank of the big creek while he looked for a place to cross. I suspicioned that he didn't know which side of the creek he lived on. It was getting dark, so I said, 'Now look, sonny, it'll be dark in a minute, and I don't know where you live, so if you'll come home with me tonight we'll go to your house first thing in the morning.' I knew that if I got to wandering around in the thick woods that late I'd get lost too." Mr. London twisted his cap and looked at the men.

"Yes, yes," Papa said.

"He was powerful hard to persuade, and suddenly he saw this swinging footbridge and he started running to it, just like he knowed it was there all the time." Mr. London shook his head. "The water

looked powerful deep and cold to me, and the rope cables on that bridge looked powerful rotten. I was afraid they might break, but the boy was already halfway across and I felt like I had to risk it for the boy's sake. But when we got across, I could tell he didn't know which way to turn, so I said, 'Now, sonny, let's go thisaway,' and we kept close to the big creek so I wouldn't get lost in strange country. Mind you, I don't lose my way that easy, but I'm new in these parts and it was getting powerful dark."

"You did the right thing," Papa said. "But in all this time, didn't you hear a gunshot or a horn?"

Mr. London shook his head. "No, sir. I don't recall any. But don't forget that we was way over yonder."

Papa nodded. "Now, you crossed the creek. Then what?"

"Well, sir, as luck would have it, we came out in the road just this side of my house."

Again Theron stepped up. "And Charles didn't know where he was?"

"Son, it was powerful dark by now," Mr. London said. "And that fog was so thick you could feel it. I recollect saying to the boy, 'It's as black as a stack o' panthers out here.' And about that time your brother bumped into me and I could tell he was so scared he was sick. He kept saying he lived five, maybe ten, miles over thataway . . . The boy needs sleep;

wouldn't go to bed last night. Course, we're not fixed up very comfortable yet, but he could have slept with my three little boys."

"Oh, you have three boys?" Papa said.

"Yes, sir, three boys and three girls. Two girls older, then the baby's a girl. Like I say, your boy wouldn't go to bed. Huddled by the fireplace all night. I sort of slept with one eye open. Kept the fire built up so he wouldn't get too cold. Then, too, I feared he might get a notion to leave in the middle of the night. He sure was taking it hard. Kept saying, 'Mama's worryin' about me.'

"I reckon I was right," Mr. London continued. "Because when the first little ray of light showed, he got up and slipped out, quiet as a Indian. I jumped in my shoes and tore out to catch him, but he was just astanding there. He said, 'Does this house face the west?' and I said 'Yes' and he said, 'I live right up there in the first house on the other side of the road,' and he broke into a run and I had a hard time keeping up with him. I had to come along just to make sure he was right and that he didn't get lost again."

"You did the right thing, Mr. London," Papa said. "And we're mighty beholden to you."

"I know the boy dozed some after midnight," Mr. London said. "And I reckon along toward morning his bearings came back to him."

"Exactly," Papa said.

"Let's go, Ketcherside," Mr. Dickson said. "You go spread the word that we don't need a search party after all, and I'll go to the woods and tell Rossman."

As the men turned to go, Papa said, "We're mighty beholden to you men, too. Tell the others the same goes for them."

"Glad to help out, Holliway," one of the men said.

Again Mr. London tried to go, but Papa urged him to stay longer. "We were just fixing to eat," Papa said. "Come have breakfast with us."

"Oh, no, sir." Mr. London looked very pained. "I'll get back to the missus and the children."

"Well now, wait just a minute." Papa pulled at his ear and looked into the fire. "You say you were out yesterday hunting game for Christmas dinner. Did you get any?"

"Only the squirrel." Mr. London forced a smile. "Better luck next time."

"Well, you know it just might be that we can fix that," Papa said.

Mama had come back in the front room and she was standing quietly to one side. "I was thinking the same thing, so I fixed you a little something." She and Millie started for the kitchen, then Mama paused and asked, "Do you have a cow, sir?"

Mr. London twisted his cap. "No, ma'am, not yet. I plan to buy one, but . . ."

Mama hurried on, with Millie right behind her. She grabbed a gallon syrup bucket, poured it full of the fresh morning milk and put on the lid. She had put the rest of the ham, a pound of butter, and a loaf of bread in a box and now she took the box and the milk and gave them to Mr. London. Papa opened the door.

"I'm much obliged to you, ma'am," Mr. London said as he went out.

"We're much obliged to you, sir," Mama said. "Merry Christmas, and God bless you all."

On the steps, Mr. London turned back. "You've got a fine son, ma'am. But he's had a powerful bad shock. He'll get over it quicker if you don't make him talk about it."

"We won't," Mama promised.

"That's right," Papa said. "If it's ever talked about in this household the boy will have to bring it up himself. Good day to you, sir." Papa closed the door.

Millie ran to the kitchen and looked out the window. It was full daylight now, and Charles was out between the squirrel and raccoon cages, tossing bits of sausage and biscuit to Trixie and Blue.

"Goodness, I'm starving," Miss May exclaimed.

"Me, too," Millie chimed in.

They gathered around the table. Papa must have forgotten that he had already asked the breakfast grace; anyhow, he asked another one. And this time he mentioned Charles by name and thanked God for keeping him safe. The sausages were crisper than usual and the biscuits were hard, but Millie thought this was the best breakfast she had ever eaten.

Later Charles came in the front room with Rickey on his shoulder. He stopped at the fireplace, and

Rickey, turning upside down, clung to Charles's clothing with his hind paws and reached in the pockets of his overalls for the crumbs of biscuit and sausage.

Charles plopped down on the braided rug and looked at the Christmas tree. "Say, how come this coon hasn't eaten the popcorn off the tree?" he asked.

"Because I watched him all day yesterday," Ruth said.

Charles grew serious. "Mama, did you have any popcorn left?"

"No, son, but I can pop some more. Why?"

"Well," Charles said slowly, "I think those little kids down yonder sure would like to have some."

Papa leaned forward in his chair and said, "We wondered, son, but you never know just how far to go without hurting a man's pride."

Charles tickled Rickey's ear before saying, "Hungry little kids don't have pride, Papa."

"What did they have to eat last night, son?" Mama asked.

Charles kept his head bowed low as he said, "A squirrel and some water gravy."

Mama closed her eyes and her lips moved. Papa rose, saying, "I'm going to hitch the team to the wagon, Sarah. Get some things together for them."

Mama and Millie started to the kitchen. "Mama,"

Charles called, "if you have an extra quilt they sure could use it."

"Yes, son." Mama hurried on. She sent Theron to the smokehouse for a slab of meat. Then she found a box and packed a cake, two pies, a bag of potatoes, and some dried peaches.

"Oh, the quilts," she said. She got two heavy comforters that she had made by covering old quilts with the good parts of worn-out overalls. Mama never wasted anything. She either made it over for someone else to wear or she put it in a quilt or a rug or something.

Papa had stopped the wagon at the back fence, and now he and Theron came into the house. Each carried a crate, and Papa carried a bucket also. Millie and Ruth squealed, for they knew immediately what was in the crates and bucket. It just wouldn't be Christmas without them.

"We went down in the cellar to get some canned goods for the Londons," Papa teased the girls, "and just look what we found. I reckon Santa Claus came last night and when he saw the lights in the house, he just left things in the cellar."

Ruth pounded Papa with her fists. Millie grabbed the hammer off the mantel and Papa pulled the nails out of the crates.

Charles looked up and said, "Why didn't somebody hang up the stockings last night?"

"Well," Millie grinned and cast her eyes at Charles, "you were the only thing we really wanted for Christmas, and we didn't think Santa could put you in a stocking."

Papa had the lids off the crates and bucket, and was handing out apples and oranges. He let each one choose his own candy.

"Send some of every kind of candy to the London children, Mama," Charles suggested.

"We're doing just that," Mama said, dipping it out with the sugar scoop into a brown paper bag.

As they helped Papa carry things to the wagon, Mama said, "John, tell the man to come every day and get a bucket of milk for the children, and tell the woman I'll pay her a visit later."

"Yes," Papa said. As he drove down the road toward the Londons' house, Mama shook her head.

"The Lord works in strange ways to show us what needs to be done," she said. "It's awful what we all went through, but if Charles hadn't got lost, those poor children might not have had a bite to eat on Christmas Day."

Millie ran into the house and gave Charles a squeeze before the rest of the family came in. Then they shoved each other back, laughed, and started playing with Rickey.

There had been so much excitement that Millie never knew when Miss May put on another ham to

bake. But when it came time to eat the Christmas dinner, there it was, all brown and glazed on the outside
and lean and tender on the inside. And there were
more cakes and pies and good things than they
could possibly eat in one day.

"Oh," Millie said as they gathered around the
table, "this is a Christmas to remember."

Papa Goes to School

Millie stood at the front window looking out. She and Ruth would go back to school in the morning, and she didn't know whether to be happy or unhappy about it. Every time she thought of school she saw Miss Comstock's white face with the penetrating black eyes and the thin mouth set in a downward curve. If things didn't straighten out between her and the teacher, she didn't see any hope of ever being really happy at this school.

Charles had come down with a high fever Christmas Day and Mama had put him to bed and rubbed his chest with a mixture of goose grease and kerosene. He wouldn't be able to start school in the morning after all, and Millie had so looked forward to it. Perhaps if Charles were in school her problem with the teacher wouldn't seem so big.

Only Millie and Miss May were in the front room. Although Miss May was sitting near the fire embroidering, Millie knew she was watching her, expecting her to take up her books and review her lessons. But somehow Millie couldn't put her mind to it.

"What's wrong, Millie?" Miss May asked abruptly.

Millie closed her eyes. "Nothing."

"Oh, come now, you know you can't fool me." Miss May put her work aside. "Something's had you down ever since I came. Now come and tell me about it."

Keeping her face turned away, Millie struggled to control her voice. "The teacher . . . doesn't . . . like me."

"The teacher doesn't like you?"

Millie shook her head.

"Oh, child, you must be imagining things. Why doesn't the teacher like you?"

"I don't know," Millie choked.

"Come here." Miss May motioned Millie to her side. "If the teacher doesn't like you there's a reason for it. Now why?"

"I don't know," Millie insisted. "Unless it's . . . because . . ."

"Because what?"

"Because I'm the littlest one in the sixth grade."

Miss May frowned. "What difference does that

make? Somebody has to be the littlest, just as somebody has to be the biggest."

"Wel-l-l, there's more to it than that," Millie admitted. "Miss Comstock thinks I'm too little to know anything or do anything or—or something. Like when I told her I made my dress and Ruth's. She called me a—she said I was—well, she didn't believe it."

"Oh, Mil-l-ie, child. Don't you see what you've done? You've dared to be different. You've dared to do your best, to be a little above the average, and when you do that you're bound to be misunderstood by some people. But don't let it turn you from your course." Miss May looked at her kindly but seriously. "A body has to be a little out of the ordinary in order to do anything really special. Don't you see? Now stop worrying about it, and go right on doing your best. Why, I'll bet if you only knew it, your teacher loves you and admires you a lot."

"I doubt that," Millie said. "But it does help, just knowing that somebody else knows about it."

"Sakes alive, child, you should have told me when I first came. Why, your parents could have helped you if you had told them."

But Millie didn't see any need to bother Mama and Papa. Already she felt better, and she hoped Miss May would not mention it to the rest of the family. She began arranging her books.

Ruth came in, dropped down on the braided rug and tickled Rickey's ear with a broom straw.

"Ruth," Miss May said, "does it seem to you that your schoolteacher doesn't like Millie?"

Millie gasped.

"Sure," Ruth said. "Everybody knows that."

Just then Papa came in at the front door with some firewood. "Everybody knows what, Ruthie?" he asked.

Millie clutched the edge of the standtable. Ruth bowed her head and scooted out of Papa's way. Papa laid the wood on the fire, brushed himself off and said, "Papa spoke to you, Ruthie, and you didn't answer."

Millie wanted to run, but she knew better. Keeping her face down Ruth said, "Everybody knows Miss Comstock hates Millie."

"What?" Mama said, coming into the room. She had decided that Charles was able to dress and come sit by the fire awhile. And right behind Mama and Charles was Theron. Suddenly the whole family knew about Millie's trouble.

"What did you say, Ruth?" Papa demanded.

"I said . . . everybody knows . . . Miss Comstock hates Millie." Ruth covered her face with her hands.

"Why?" they all wanted to know.

Ruth dug at her eyes. "Because she thinks she's a smart aleck."

"A what?"

They all looked at Millie.

"Just a minute," Miss May said, putting up both hands. "I don't think it's that way at all. It's just that there's been a misunderstanding."

Miss May tried to explain, but Mama and Papa wanted to know why Millie hadn't told them, and

Millie tried to explain she hadn't thought it was important enough. The more they talked the more tangled things became until finally Papa said, "Well, if a daughter of mine has left the impression that she's a smart aleck I intend to get to the bottom of it. I'll go to school with you girls in the morning and see what this is all about."

"No, Papa, Miss Comstock didn't say 'smart aleck.' She only said 'smartie.'" Millie was quite upset by now. "And you don't have to waste your time by going to school."

"No, Cottontop, I know I don't have to," Papa said. "But when there's a misunderstanding, the sooner it's straightened out the better."

Millie wanted to die. What would Papa say to Miss Comstock? And what would Miss Comstock say? And wouldn't everything be worse for Millie afterward than it had been before? These and dozens of other questions churned in her mind. That night she dreamed about the whole miserable situation, and she woke up the next morning desperately hoping Papa had changed his mind.

She tried to find words to persuade Papa not to go to school with her and Ruth, but no words came. Papa had spoken, and he'd do just as he'd said. And not only did he start earlier than they usually started, but he walked so fast, the girls had to trot to keep up with him. Millie hoped they'd be so early that Miss Comstock wouldn't be there, and Papa would give up and go back home.

But it wasn't a reasonable thing to hope for. Millie knew that part of the schoolteacher's job was to come early and build the first fire and sweep the floor. When they came in sight of the schoolhouse, smoke was curling out of the chimney. Millie's heart sank.

Miss Comstock looked surprised when Papa came in with the girls. Papa never was one to talk about the weather when he had something else to say, so after he had properly introduced himself he went straight to the point.

"Miss Comstock, my daughter Millie here seems to think you don't like her. And I say if that's the case, then she's done something to give you a reason. I'm here to see if we can get it straightened out."

Millie closed her eyes and held her breath.

"What makes her think that?" Miss Comstock asked.

"Maybe she can answer that better than I can," Papa said. He looked at Millie. Miss Comstock looked at her too, and Millie knew they were waiting for an answer. She felt faint.

"Well—well, you look at me like you don't like

me." Millie's chin trembled. "You almost never call on me to recite." She picked at a rough place on her fingernail.

"I can explain that," Miss Comstock said. "I don't call on you often in class because I know that you know the answers. I can tell that you have help at home. The children who are less fortunate than you, the ones who do not have help at home, are the ones who need the most attention at school, so they are the ones I call on."

Millie felt foolish for having been such a baby.

Papa turned his cap in his hands and said, "I'm

afraid there's more to it than that, Miss Comstock. According to the girls, it seems that on the first morning you called Millie a smart aleck."

Millie wanted to remind Papa that the word was "smartie," not "smart aleck," but Miss Comstock was speaking.

"Not really, Mr. Holliway. I wouldn't call a child a name. As I recall it, I said something to the effect that we didn't have time here for smarties. I didn't mean to be rude, sir. I remember that on the day Millie and Ruth started school I was rather distraught, and I'm afraid I tried too hard to be clever and gay. Every time I try to be somebody that I'm not it turns out all wrong."

Papa picked at a frayed place on his cap. "Well, ma'am, I feel awful foolish, like I've suspected a mountain when there's only a little molehill. I reckon I owe you an apology."

"Not at all, sir," Miss Comstock said. "I admire any parent who'll come to school to straighten out a misunderstanding. It is I who owe Millie an apology. And I would have apologized before now except that I kept hoping she hadn't noticed the incident."

"No, ma'am, you're wrong there," Papa said quietly. "That one doesn't miss much. We call her Cottontop, but as the old saying goes, she's got a head like a tar bucket; everything you throw at it sticks."

Miss Comstock smiled and Millie felt her face grow warm with embarrassment.

Papa said awkwardly, "You'll pardon me, ma'am, if I sound personal, but the neighbors tell me your mother has been sick for quite a spell. Could that be why you were upset the day the girls started to school?"

"Yes," Miss Comstock said. "But Mother's illness is my problem, not the children's, and I shouldn't let it affect me in the schoolroom."

"Well, what I'm trying to say is, me and my wife and a woman that's visiting us right now—Miss May, that is—have been discussing your problem. Miss May says she'll be more than glad to go over and help you out."

"Why, that's very kind of her," Miss Comstock said. "I've been trying to find someone but there just hasn't seemed to be anyone in the neighborhood who could leave her own home."

Papa nodded thoughtfully. "Maybe something can be done." He turned to go.

"Mr. Holliway," Miss Comstock said. Papa paused. "I hope you'll feel free to visit us at school any time."

"Thank you, ma'am."

The Problem Solved

A slow smile crept over Miss Comstock's face as she looked at Millie and put out her hand. Millie grabbed the hand and pressed it to her cheek.

"I'm sorry, Miss Comstock," she said. "I have acted awful, and I'm sorry."

"It's all right," Miss Comstock said, touching Millie's hair. "I'm glad it all came out in the open and it's over with. Now we can start the new year with a better understanding."

A blast of cold air hit them as someone opened the door. It was Buster Emerson's week to take care of the fire, so he had come early and was bringing in a huge load of wood.

"Good morning, Buster," Miss Comstock said cheerily.

Buster looked at her wide-eyed and dropped a stick of wood on his toe. "Ouch! Oh, how-do," he stammered.

Miss Comstock opened the stove door and Buster piled the wood in. "I—I'll go get another load so I won't have to go out during classes," he sputtered, hurrying back outside.

"Millie, there's something I meant to speak to your father about," Miss Comstock said. "Wasn't it your brother who was lost on Christmas Eve?"

"Yes, ma'am."

"But he's found now," Ruth said quickly.

"But why isn't he in school?" Miss Comstock asked.

"He's sick," Ruth said.

Millie nodded. "He was supposed to start school today."

"What grade is he in?" Miss Comstock asked.

"The seventh, I guess. He was in the sixth last year." Millie suddenly realized that Charles couldn't be sure he had passed the sixth for the same reason she hadn't known whether she had passed the fifth.

Miss Comstock smiled. "If he was in the sixth last year, I guess that makes him in the seventh this year."

Millie knew that wasn't the whole truth, but she

wanted Charles to be in the seventh grade, so she changed the subject. "Miss Comstock, there's one thing I'd like to say about Charles."

"Yes?"

"Well, the man who found him said he'd forget it quicker if we didn't talk about it, so Papa said we wouldn't ever talk about it at home. And I thought maybe if nobody made him talk about it at school . . ."

"I see," Miss Comstock said.

The door opened and several cold, red-faced children piled inside.

Miss Comstock put her hand on Millie's shoulder. "We'll see what we can do about it," she promised, turning to her desk. "Not so noisy, children." She clapped her hands together. "Sam, go close the door for Buster."

When classes had begun and Millie was settled in her seat, she thought the sun shining across her desk had never been so bright and friendly.

"Children," Miss Comstock began, "Millie has a favor to ask of the whole school, and I think right now is a good time for it."

The sudden announcement nearly shocked Millie out of her seat. Whatever was Miss Comstock talking about?

"Come to the front of the room, Millie, so everyone can hear you."

Millie slipped out of her seat and crept to the front of the room. She had no idea what she was supposed to say.

"I'm sure most of you know it was Millie's brother who was lost on Christmas Eve," Miss Comstock said. "If any of you want to ask questions, ask them now so you won't have to talk about it later."

"I know all about it," Elvira Jones said. "Papa was one of the men in the search party."

"Me, too," Willie Ketcherside declared. "Papa went to help look for him, but he was already found."

Suddenly all the children were talking at once. Miss Comstock allowed them to talk for a few minutes, then she rapped the desk with a ruler. "We can't talk about it all day," she said. "Let's let Millie ask her favor, then I want to see how many of you will do as she asks. All right, Millie."

Millie gulped. "Well, we think Charles will get over it quicker if we don't make him talk about it. So I thought, when he comes to school, if you wouldn't ask him questions maybe he wouldn't get sick again and—and have to miss more school."

"Oh, no," several children promised as Millie went back to her seat. But of course the children had not heard all they wanted to hear, so at recess and at noon they gathered around Millie and Ruth and asked endless questions.

That afternoon, just before school was out, Millie glanced up and caught Miss Comstock looking at her in that same old way, with the corners of her mouth drawn down. But this time, instead of looking away, Millie smiled. Miss Comstock smiled back, and then looked down at the papers on her desk.

"It's time to put your books away, children," Miss Comstock said. There was the usual shuffling of books and getting of coats, then the long line out to the road. When Miss Comstock said, "Dismissed," Millie waved and the teacher waved back.

Millie hurried home to tell Mama and Miss May how well things had turned out. She ran up the porch steps and started to open the door.

"Be careful, girls," Mama called. "Don't bump our quilting frame with the door."

Millie opened the door slowly and she and Ruth squeezed inside. Mama had hung the square quilting frame from the ceiling with a heavy cord at each corner, and she and Charles sat on opposite sides quilting.

"Where's Miss May?" Millie asked.

"She's gone," Charles answered.

"Gone!" Millie echoed. "Where?"

Mama explained. "When Papa came back from

school this morning, the three of us went to visit your teacher's mother. We found her bedfast, so Miss May said that since she didn't have a family of her own to care for, she'd be doing a good neighborly act to stay and take care of Mrs. Comstock. So she stayed."

Millie frowned, trying hard not to be disappointed.

Papa had just come in and sat warming his feet at the fireplace. He said, "Considering everything else your teacher had to worry about, Cottontop, it's no wonder she didn't pay you much mind. It just goes to show that we shouldn't ever judge the other fellow. We might not have all the facts, and we never know what secret burdens he might be bearing."

Millie bowed her head in shame for having been so wrapped up in herself.

At school the next morning Miss Comstock said, "Millie, were you surprised when you got home yesterday and found Miss May gone?"

"I surely was," Millie answered.

"You couldn't have been more surprised than I was when I got home and found her there," Miss Comstock admitted. "But I'm so thankful. Knowing she's there with Mother will take a great load off my mind."

"Miss May is good with sick people," Millie managed to say. Not used to talking with Miss Comstock, she found it hard to keep up her end of the conversation.

"I think we worked out a wonderful arrangement," Miss Comstock continued. "Miss May will come to our house on Monday morning and stay until the following Friday afternoon. Then she'll go back to your house for the weekend."

"Oh?" Millie was glad Miss May wasn't gone for good.

"Of course, I'll pay her," Miss Comstock explained.

"You'll be surprised at how much work Miss May can do with her crippled hands," Millie said proudly.

Charles started to school on Wednesday, and Millie was happier than she'd been in a long time. When school was out Friday afternoon, Papa was waiting in the road in the wagon. He was going to pick up Miss May, so his children and Miss Comstock rode with him. Papa also invited all the children living in that direction to climb in. There was quite a load, and Bob and Becky had to strain to start the wagon moving. Papa stopped along the way to let the children off when they reached their homes or came to a place where they cut through the woods. The wagon turned south at the first corner then back west at the next corner. And there was the picket

fence. Papa stopped at the gate and Miss Comstock
asked them to get out and come in.

"No, thank you, ma'am, not this time. We'll just
wait," Papa said.

They didn't have to wait long, for Miss May was
ready to go. When they were back home and in the
house, Millie said, "Oh, Miss May, it's good to have
you back."

"How did things go, May?" Mama asked.

"Just fine," Miss May said. "But there's no doubt

that Mrs. Comstock needs someone with her, at least
for a while."

The arrangement worked out well, and week after
week Miss May took care of Mrs. Comstock from
Monday morning until Friday afternoon. Millie
looked forward to the weekends when she and Miss
May could exchange views and talk of many things.

A Horse, a Sled, and
a Pretty Girl

The weather turned very bad—or very good, depending upon whether you were walking or sledding. It rained, then the ground froze, and on top of that came a thick layer of wet snow, which glazed over and became very slick.

Papa said a farm wasn't complete without a sled, so he helped the boys make one. It was three feet wide and five feet long and it had two-by-four runners and a sturdy bed. It would hold anything from a barrel of water to eight children. Theron and Charles could pull the sled with a light load, but it worked best with a horse. And that's where Star came in. Star was Becky's colt. All his life he had been petted and patted, and lately the boys had been putting him in harness.

One afternoon the children were slipping and sliding all over the road on their way home from school. For the most part they enjoyed the ice, but Ruth had taken so many falls that she was about to cry. She begged Charles to carry her books.

"Oh, Ruthie, don't be such a baby," Millie said. Just then her feet flew up and her arms flew out and she was flat on the ice. The dinner bucket rolled into the ditch and her books and papers scattered about. The other children doubled up with laughter.

"Wow!" Millie said, getting to her feet. She gathered up her belongings and took it more cautiously the rest of the way home.

Theron had Star hitched to the sled and was out in the road.

"Reckon he'll let us ride?" Charles asked.

"I think so," Theron answered. "Come and let's try him."

Ruth went inside, but Millie and Charles left their books on the porch and went back out with Theron.

"You'd better hang on tight, Millie," Theron cautioned. "He might take a sudden notion to run." Millie stood between her brothers and clung to the brace across the front of the sled.

Down the road they went, Star's hoofs clickety-clacking on the ice, and the wind whipping their faces. Near the roadside a tree branch cracked under its burden of ice and crashed to the ground. Star shot forward like a bullet. It happened so fast that Theron dropped one of the reins and the horse swerved out of the middle of the road.

Millie clutched the brace while Charles and Theron grabbed wildly for the loose rein. The sled was all the way out of the road now, and the ditch alongside the road was growing steeper as they approached Muddy Boggy Creek. Crystal splinters of ice, off dead weeds and grass, flew in all directions as they sped along.

The ditch grew deeper and the creek came nearer. There was no railing across the bridge, and the sled was so far off the road that one runner was sure to miss the edge. And if that happened, they'd all be thrown into the creek. For that matter, Star might miss the bridge entirely.

"The creek, Theron!" Millie screamed.

Theron jabbed her hard with his elbow. "Don't scream!" he said between clenched teeth. "You'll scare him worse."

Millie looked for a place to jump.

"Don't jump, Millie!" Theron shouted. "You'll break your neck. Hang on!"

Charles leaned way out over the side of the bouncing sled, caught the flapping rein and pulled hard. Just in time they guided Star back up into the road and over the bridge. The boys pulled hard and steady on the reins.

"Whoa, boy. Whoa, boy," they coaxed. Star began to slow down. When he finally stopped, his flanks were quivering.

"Whoa, boy." Theron took the reins and Charles climbed off the sled to soothe the frightened horse. Millie's tongue felt as if it had needles in it and her knees were so weak that she sat down.

"You think we'd better walk back?" Charles asked.

"No," Theron said. "He just got scared. He'll be all right now."

They turned the horse around and started back home at a slower pace. Theron wrapped the reins around his hands for a better grip.

As they rode along, Millie asked, "Theron, do you suppose Papa would let you take us to school in the sled in the morning?"

"I don't know, but we'll ask him. I don't have anything special to do, and the exercise would be good for Star."

Papa did allow Theron to take the children to school on the sled the next morning, but he cautioned Theron not to take a load of children for a ride. "The colt might take a notion to run again," Papa said, "and somebody might get hurt."

Charles and Theron stood up front and Millie and Ruth sat down on the sled. At school they proudly showed off Star. Even Miss Comstock came out and admired him.

After a few moments the teacher asked, "Why aren't you coming to school, Theron?"

Theron looked down and wound the reins around his hands. "Oh, I don't know," he said. "Reckon I'd feel out of place, big as I am and all."

"As for size, you could pass for a grown man," Miss Comstock said. "But getting an education is important. We have boys older and bigger than you in school, and we'd be happy to have you, too."

Theron didn't seem to know what to say.

"You think about it," Miss Comstock suggested. "An education is a mighty good thing to have." She went back into the schoolhouse.

Jane Rossman had been stroking Star's neck. Now she stepped up and Millie introduced her.

"Hi," Theron said awkwardly. "It was your father that helped us look for—" Theron caught himself. "I mean, I've met your father."

Charles interrupted. "He means it was your father that stayed out in the woods all night with Papa when I was lost. I don't know why everybody acts like they do. Anybody can get lost. I'm lucky I got found."

That afternoon Theron came back and was waiting out in the road when school was out. He offered Jane a ride and she stood up front between him and Charles. Millie and Ruth sat toward the back of the sled. When they reached the place where Jane cut across the field, Theron stopped to let her off. "Reckon you'll freeze before you get home?" he asked.

"Maybe not." Jane smiled, and ran.

Theron shook the reins and Star took off so suddenly that Millie and Ruth clutched at each other.

"You know, Charles," Theron said, "I just might start to school after all."

Millie was about to jump up and encourage Theron, but Charles chuckled and said, "She is pretty, isn't she?"

Theron grinned. "Aw, I don't think a woman's worth it."

But in the following weeks Millie was pleased to notice that Theron and Jane became very good friends. One day she heard Theron say to Charles, "I hope Papa doesn't move from this place next fall. I think Jane and I are going to get along fine."

Millie hoped Papa wouldn't move, too, but her reasons were different from Theron's. Now that she and Miss Comstock understood each other, school was a happy experience, and she found herself hoping she could stay long enough to finish both seventh and eighth grades here.

One evening in early March, Mama had Theron take her to visit the Londons. Ever since Christmas, Mr. London had been coming every night for a bucket of fresh milk, but he hadn't come for two nights now. Mama was afraid he might be sick. When she and Theron returned, saying the Londons had moved out, Papa said maybe they had gone to kinfolks somewhere who could help them. Millie thought about the tall, thin, strange man. What would have happened to Charles if this stranger hadn't found him? Wherever the Londons were, Millie hoped they were comfortable and had plenty to eat.

A Hidden Message

One Friday night Papa said he needed to go to town the next day.

"Good," Miss May said quickly. "I'll just let you take me home."

Millie's hand went over her mouth. She didn't want Miss May to go.

"Mrs. Comstock has improved so much that she can go outside and feed the chickens," Miss May said. "So of course they don't really need me any longer. This way I'll get home in time to plant a late garden."

Mama nodded. "I'll go visit Mrs. Comstock as often as I can."

The next morning they gathered up all of Miss May's belongings, and Mama put in a few extras— some dried peaches, hominy, and a stick of the smoked sausage. Papa helped Miss May into the spring seat, and Millie stood on the porch and waved good-by.

That first weekend was lonesome without Miss May. It always was.

While Millie had been busy making the best grades possible, spring had popped out everywhere. The blossoming peach orchard looked like a pink cloud hanging just above the ground. Baby chickens, turkeys, ducks, and goslings were all about the place.

The raccoon had grown to full size, and now that the days were warmer he almost never came in the house. He wore a leather collar, and when he wasn't in his cage he was chained to the clothesline, where he could run back and forth. Sometimes a visiting dog dared to pick a fight with Rickey, but the dog always got the worst of it and left the yard yelping.

The squirrels, too, had grown. Millie often walked about the place with all three of them clinging to her. The only thing wrong with them was that the two males sometimes fought bitterly. Millie tried to separate them once, but that was one time too many. With blood dripping from her hands, she ran into the house.

"Dear me, child!" Mama exclaimed. "You look like a squirrel has had ahold of you."

"It was that ole big one," Millie wailed. "Charles is going to have to do something about him." She washed her hands in warm soapy water and gritted her teeth as Mama painted the scratches with iodine. "Wow, that burns!" she said.

But Charles didn't have to do anything about the squirrel. When Millie went back outside to put them in the cage the big one bounded up a tree. Frantically, Millie tried to coax him down with corn and nuts, but he jumped from that tree to the next and then the next. The oak trees were covered with leaves now so that Millie soon lost sight of the squirrel.

Whatever would she do? Charles loved the squirrels, and he had worked so patiently to capture and tame them. There was nothing to do but tell Charles the truth. When he came in from the field she explained what had happened.

"Let him go," Charles said. "He's too mean to worry about. And besides, we'll soon have some baby squirrels."

Charles was right. A few days later one of the squirrels refused to come out of the hollow log to eat. The next day the children discovered that she had a nest of babies.

"Oh, when can we see them?" the girls wanted to know.

"You'd better not put your hand in there," Charles warned.

"Don't worry!" Millie looked at the brown scratches on her hands.

But Charles had a way with animals. That night when he fed them, the mother came out of the nest and he reached in and felt three babies. He let Millie hold one of them for just a moment. The baby squirrel was not much bigger than her thumb. Its naked little body was as smooth as silk and it looked all tail and legs.

"Here, let's put him back before he gets chilled," Charles said. "We'll have to build them a wheel to play on when they get bigger."

In the afternoon of the last day of school, Miss Comstock gave the higher grades their last assignment in writing. It was a single sentence written on the blackboard, and each pupil was to copy it over and over until he had filled a whole page. The sentence read: A DIAMOND IN THE ROUGH IS A DIAMOND SURE ENOUGH.

Millie began writing, carefully dotting her *i*'s, crossing her *t*'s, and making the humps on her *m*'s and *n*'s. She was proud of her handwriting, and she certainly wanted her last grade to be a good one. Over and over she wrote the sentence. She was half-way down the page when she stopped suddenly and looked at the blackboard as if seeing it for the first time. She looked at Miss Comstock, sitting at her desk signing report cards. This was not just an assignment in writing; this was a message the teacher wanted the children to get.

Resting her elbows on her desk and her chin on her fists, Millie looked right through the freckle on Buster Emerson's neck.

"You have three minutes to finish, children," Miss Comstock said.

Millie jumped and began writing faster than before. The last lines were not as neat as the first ones, but now she knew that perfect penmanship was not the most important point. Miss Comstock rose, picked up her pointer, and stepped to the blackboard. "All right, what have you written?" she asked, tapping the board. "All together, read it to me."

In unison, the children from the fifth grade up read, "A diamond in the rough is a diamond sure enough."

Miss Comstock turned from the board and said, "Boys and girls, if you haven't learned another thing this year, I want you to get this one lesson. A diamond looks like nothing but a rock when it's taken from the earth. It is only through hard work and polishing that its true value is revealed. And that's the way it is with you children. You are now like uncut diamonds. But with hard work and planning you can become truly valuable citizens. It is within the reach of each one of you to become a diamond in your own right. Only one person on earth can keep you from it, and that person is *you*. Only one person can make a diamond of you, and that person is *you*. Whatever you choose as your life work, from ditch digger to President of the United States, you can succeed in that work if you strive to do it better than anyone has ever done it before."

For a moment the room was so quiet that when a first-grader dropped his pencil it sounded like a stick of stovewood. Millie was still trying to make the dream crystallize in her mind when Miss Comstock began passing out report cards.

Beginning with the first, and working up through the grades, Miss Comstock called out the names and the children marched to the teacher's desk. They took their cards and returned to their seats. Millie waited tensely as the line of children flowed to and from the teacher's desk. Eventually her name was called. Her mouth was dry and her knees were shaky as she followed close behind Buster.

"Thank you," she breathed, taking her card.

"You're welcome." Miss Comstock smiled.

On the way back to her seat, Millie read the line: *Passed to the seventh grade.* She closed her eyes and pressed the card to her cheek. It was the first time in her life that she had gone to the very last day of school and gotten a report card showing that she had passed to the next grade. Regardless of where they lived next year, she could walk right up to the teacher and truthfully say she was in the seventh grade. She marched to her seat as proud as a princess.

Millie turned her report card over and there on the back, in a beautiful hand, Miss Comstock had written: *Millie, you have been a fine student and you*

*have made the highest average grade in your class. I
hope to see you next fall. Miss Beatrice Comstock.*

Millie hid her face in her hands to keep anyone
from seeing how overcome she was. How could she
tell Miss Comstock that she meant to be a diamond,
regardless of how rough the circumstances might
ever be? Could she make Papa understand that they
simply had to live here for at least two more years,
until she had finished the eighth grade? That night
she could scarcely control her feelings as she showed
her family her report card.

Millie's Decision

Millie faced the summer with a happiness that she had not known before. It was as if she had reached the peak of a very high mountain. And although she didn't know what lay beyond, she felt secure in the knowledge that she could start the seventh grade next fall without any feelings of guilt.

The days were warm, and while Papa and the boys cultivated the fields, Mama and the girls managed the house and worked in the garden. They made sauerkraut from the large, firm heads of cabbage, and they picked and canned vegetables, wild berries and other fruits.

Each Sunday they went to the schoolhouse to study a Bible lesson and to worship God. Millie thought Sunday was the happiest day of the week. Not only did she learn from the Bible, but she also saw Miss

Comstock and her other friends. And the Holliways either went home with some family for Sunday dinner or someone came home with them.

One day after Sunday meeting Mr. Ketcherside walked up to Papa with a very satisfied look on his face. "Holliway, you recollect that panther scare that got out last winter?" he asked.

"Not likely ever to forget it," Papa answered.

"Well, sir, I got a few bad marks 'ginst my honesty over that." Mr. Ketcherside took his hand out of his pocket and held it toward Papa. "But looky here. What you say to this?"

Papa took a small white object out of Mr. Ketcherside's hand and studied it. "Looks like a big dog or maybe wolf tooth," he said.

"Nope. Not dog, not wolf," Mr. Ketcherside said. "Panther."

"Panther!" Everybody was interested.

"Where did you get this, Sam?" Papa asked.

"'Bout fifteen miles south of here," Mr. Ketcherside said. "In town the other day I heard that a man living down this side of where Muddy Boggy flows into Clear Boggy had killed a panther last spring. So I took off and went to see for myself. Sure 'nuf, it's the truth. They've got the hide on the floor fer a rug and the head's ahangin' in the barn."

Papa ran his tongue over his lips. "Sam, I reckon I

owe you an apology. I'll have to admit I didn't put much stock in that tale when it was going around last winter."

The children all wanted to handle the panther tooth, and when Charles took it he showed his teeth and growled. "I'm sure glad I didn't have to spend last Christmas Eve in the woods with you."

One Saturday in late July, Papa came home from Atoka and said a revival meeting was starting there the next day and that they would go. The meeting would last for two weeks.

"Oh, I'm glad," Mama said. "I thought surely there'd be a gospel meeting somewhere that we could go to this summer."

Millie would soon be thirteen, and for a long time she'd been thinking about being baptized. She knew the Scriptures, for Mama and Papa had taught her all her life. That night after she went to bed the words of Mark 16:16 went round and round in her mind. *He that believeth and is baptized shall be saved; but he that believeth not shall be damned.* There was no doubt about it; she wanted to be saved.

Early Sunday morning they fried two chickens and baked a big peach cobbler. Papa said Miss May had insisted that the family go home with her for dinner, and Mama said it would be too much for all of them to go in on one person without taking something along.

Later, as Mama and the girls dressed for church, Millie said, "Mama, may I take some extra clothes? I'd like to be baptized today."

"Why, Millie, I think that's a fine decision," Mama said. "Of course we'll take you some extra clothes."

Millie wore her white dress and long white stockings and took along the brown dress with the little yellow flowers to put on afterward. She was very nervous, but she tried to control herself so that no one would notice.

The children sat on a folded quilt in the back end of the wagon, their feet swinging out. It was a long way to Atoka and the sun was hot. The wheels stirred up the dry sand, and it sifted down in thin streams. Millie hoped her white dress wouldn't get dirty before they got there.

As they neared town, a two-seated buggy loaded with people and drawn by a pair of fine bay horses turned a corner and began following them. Houses with clean-swept yards and neat flower beds appeared on both sides of the road. Now and then they passed little groups of people walking to church.

Guiding the horses off the street, Papa stopped them in the shade of a tree. The family got out and went inside a white frame building with the words

CHURCH OF CHRIST over the door. Two men met them near the door and introduced themselves. Brother James was an average-sized man with kind blue eyes and lots of wavy gray hair. Brother Daws was a large Indian with clear, dark skin and very dark eyes. After visiting briefly with the two men, the Holliways found an empty bench near the front. No sooner had Millie sat down than someone nudged her, and a little cry of joy escaped her as she looked up at Miss May.

"You all are coming home with me for dinner," Miss May said quietly.

"Yes, I know," Millie whispered.

When the service began, it was Brother Daws who led the singing. After announcing the number, he boomed "When the trumpet of the Lord shall sound and time shall be no more" with such volume it nearly lifted Millie out of her seat. And the sincere quality of his voice sent little shivers all over her. She threw her whole being into the song with the rest of the congregation.

After several songs, a man in the front row led a long prayer. Then Brother James went to the pulpit, opened his Bible and began reading. *When Jesus came into the coasts of Caesarea Philippi, he asked his disciples, saying, Whom do men say that I the Son of man am?*

Even before the preacher said so, Millie knew he was beginning his text with Matthew 16:13. He read on. *And I say also unto thee, That thou art Peter, and upon this rock I will build my church; and the gates of hell shall not prevail against it.*

Brother James talked on and Millie listened intently. Near the end of his sermon he said, "In the last verse of Acts 2 we read, *And the Lord added to the church daily such as should be saved.*" He paused. "If you want to be saved, He will add you to the church the same way today that He added people then. Will you come while we stand and sing the invitation song?" He motioned with upturned hands.

Millie trembled at the seriousness of the big step she was about to take.

"Will you come?" The preacher pleaded, his hands outstretched.

Millie bit her lower lip.

The people sang, "Trust and obey, for there's no other way to be happy in Jesus, but to trust and obey."

Millie held her breath as she slipped past Miss May into the aisle and hurried down to the front. She laid her hand in Brother James's and he eased her onto the front seat, where she sat quietly while the singing continued and while others came. She didn't know how long the singing lasted or how many came, but

eventually Brother James came back to her, asked her to stand and then asked, "Do you believe that Jesus Christ is the Son of the living God?"

"I do," Millie said distinctly.

"May God bless you in that confession," Brother James said. "It's the same one the Ethiopian made when Philip baptized him beside the road to Gaza."

Millie nodded, remembering the story in the eighth chapter of Acts. Brother James moved on to the others who had come for baptism, asking them the same question and giving them words of encouragement.

After communion and the close of the service, a crowd of people went to a creek at the edge of town. Millie shook as if she had a chill. Mama and Miss May took her black patent-leather slippers off and pinned the hem of her dress to her white stockings to keep it from floating up in the water.

"Are you cold, Millie?" Miss May asked.

"No." Millie tried to smile, and she tried hard to keep from shaking but she couldn't. Mama wrapped a quilt around her and held her close until it was her turn to walk out into the water to meet Brother James. The preacher's grasp was gentle but firm, and Millie was not afraid as they walked out and the water crept up to her armpits. They stopped and Brother James explained that he would hold a folded handkerchief over her nose when he put her under the water. Then they turned and faced the crowd on the creek bank. She clutched his left wrist while he said a short prayer. Then gently he laid her back until the water closed over her and just as gently raised her up again.

Millie heard the people on the bank singing, "Happy day, happy day, When Jesus washed my sins away." Brother James led her back to shallow water. As she stepped out onto dry ground, Mama wrapped the quilt around her and they went into the home of a woman living nearby.

When Mama and Miss May had helped her out of her wet clothes and into her dry ones, Mama kissed her and said, "Millie, you're a Christian now, and may you always wear the name with reverence and quiet dignity."

Millie smiled. Miss May put her arms about her and said, "You're not shaking so much now. Do you feel better?"

"Oh, yes," Millie said. "This is the happiest day of my life. And somehow I feel cleaner than I've ever felt before."

One Wonderful Thing
at a Time

The revival meeting in town closed the first Sunday in August. The Holliways had gone all three Sundays and a few nights. When it was over, Millie felt like a different person—as if she were a part of everything and yet more of an individual than she had ever been before. She couldn't explain it, except that she felt good inside.

The work on the farm went on. Mama said the first thing she and the girls had to get at was drying the peaches and apples. They picked bucketfuls of luscious red peaches and sat under the shade trees in the yard and carefully cut them in half and removed the seeds. Then Mama placed the fruit, cut side up, on a clean sheet weighted down with flat rocks on top of the lean-to. Here the fruit would dry and shrivel and turn brown in the hot sun, and

Mama would have lots of dried fruit for delicious pies next winter.

While Mama spread out the fruit, Millie went to the orchard for another bucketful. She climbed a tree to reach some especially good-looking peaches, and as she was about to jump down Blue barked furiously.

Millie caught herself and looked down. There on the ground where she would have jumped was a huge snake. She watched in terrified silence as the diamondback rattler jerked itself into an S curve for a strike. Its tail was off the ground and its rattles were whirring. Millie clung to the tree.

Blue stood spraddle-legged a few feet from the snake. He barked, and the snake struck. Blue ran around the tree and barked again from the other side. The snake struck again. Then, as it was pulling itself into another series of curves, Blue charged in and grabbed it just behind the head. He shook it, turned it loose, grabbed it again and shook and shook. Then quickly Blue ran his mouth up and down the length of the snake, biting it through with each snap of his jaws. When at last he let it go, the snake writhed helplessly.

Weak and trembling, Millie climbed down. She grabbed her bucket of peaches and ran to the house. Mama saw her running and called from the housetop, "Millie, what's wrong?"

Millie tried to control her voice lest she upset Mama and cause her to fall off the house. "It's all right, Mama," she panted. "I just got scared at a snake."

But when Mama was safely down on the ground, Millie told the whole story. Mama's face went white and she just stood and looked at Millie with her mouth open.

Panting hard, Blue ran up and stood by Millie. "You know, boy," she said, patting his head, "I didn't much like you at first. But it was only because Theron traded Bulger for you. But I can tell you one thing: from now on you're going to be one of my best friends." The young dog licked her hand.

After they had finished canning and drying fruit and making apple butter, Mama and the girls picked black-eyed peas. They spread the wagon sheet on the ground, emptied the peas onto it, and flailed them with long poles to shell them. As they winnowed out the husks, Millie asked Mama if she thought they would be moving again this fall.

"Dear me, child," Mama said, "let's not even talk about moving. I really don't know what your father will do about it."

That evening as the family sat out on the porch Millie said, "Papa, will we be starting school on the first day this year?"

Papa had started to stretch and yawn, but when she said that, he stopped and dropped his arms in his lap. Millie's heart pounded as she waited.

Slowly Papa said, "Seems like school means an awful lot to you."

"Well, we don't usually live where it would be so easy to go on the first day," Millie said. "And since we never have, I thought it would be kind of nice this year."

Papa rubbed his cheek. "What do you think, Sarah?"

"I'd be glad for them to go," Mama answered.

Millie held her breath while Papa's rocking chair creaked with his shifting. Eventually he said, "Well, I see no reason why you shouldn't."

"Oh, Papa, thank you," Millie cried.

When the girls had gone to their bedroom, Millie exclaimed, "Oh, Ruth, isn't it wonderful! Just think, I'll be in the seventh grade. And by starting the very first day, I ought to make better grades than I did last year."

Then, more to herself than to Ruth, she said, "And if Papa will only stay here two more years I can finish the eighth grade and be ready for high school." She'd like to go back outside and hear Papa say he'd do just that, but she decided against pressing him for an answer right now. After all, one wonderful thing at a time was enough.

BESSIE HOLLAND HECK was born on a farm near Colgate, Oklahoma, and now lives in Tulsa. In addition to being the busy mother of five children, she has been a free-lance writer since 1946. Her first book, MILLIE, placed second in the 1963 Sequoyah Children's Book Awards. This was followed by THE HOPEFUL YEARS, a sequel to MILLIE, set in the time of the First World War, and CACTUS KEVIN, her first book for boys, a story of rural life set in the latter years of the Second World War. All her books have an Oklahoma background, which Mrs. Heck portrays with vivid authenticity.

With THE YEAR AT BOGGY, Mrs. Heck goes back to the story of Millie, to the "quiet post-pioneer period to give emphasis to a way of life during a period of great transition." She says, "this period is as much a part of our American heritage as any since the Pilgrims landed."

ABOUT THE ARTIST

PAUL FRAME was born in Ryderwood, Maryland. He lives in New York City with his wife and two daughters. Mr. Frame attended Columbia University in New York City and began his career as a fashion artist for a large department store. He is now a freelance artist and does magazine and advertising art, but takes particular pleasure in illustrating children's books.